11, 2005

JEAN COULTHARD: A LIFE IN MUSIC

Presented to Natalie Rogerson
on the occasion of her
successful participation of
Contemporary Showcase Festival.

Congratulations!

Janet Fothergill & Wendy Potter

Jean Coulthard

A LIFE IN MUSIC

William Bruneau
& David Gordon Duke

RONSDALE

RONSDALE PRESS
3350 West 21st Avenue
Vancouver, B.C., Canada V6S 1G7
www.ronsdalepress.com

Typesetting: Julie Cochrane, in New Baskerville 11 pt on 13.5
Cover Design: Julie Cochrane
Cover Photo: Andreas Poulsson, "Jean Coulthard" (1972)
Frontispiece: John Vanderpant (1884–1939), "Jean Coulthard"
Paper: Rolland opaque cream — totally chlorine-free and acid-free

Ronsdale Press wishes to thank the Canada Council for the Arts, the Government of Canada through the Book Publishing Industry Development Program (BPIDP), and the Province of British Columbia through the British Columbia Arts Council for their support of its publishing program.

Library and Archives Canada Cataloguing in Publication

Bruneau, William A., 1944–
Jean Coulthard : a life in music / William Bruneau, David Gordon Duke. — 1st ed.

ISBN 1-55380-023-0

1. Coulthard, Jean, 1908– I. Duke, David Gordon, 1950– II. Title.

ML410.C845B89 2005 780'.92 C2005-900258-1

Printed in Canada by AGMV Marquis, Quebec

for

Dylan Andreas Uhrich

& Carolyn Kate Uhrich,

Jean Coulthard's great-grandchildren

CONTENTS

PREFACE

ALL COMPOSERS BEGIN as regional artists, before the lucky few step onto the international stage.

Born during Vancouver's pioneer beginnings, Jean Coulthard lived to participate in its busy and prosperous twenty-first century. Her life as citizen, parent, and grandparent intersected with the politics and the social development of a growing and increasingly wealthy city.

Coulthard's musical career paralleled the development of her country and city. (Coulthard pronounced her name "coal-thard," with "th" as in think, and "d" as in dark — syllables equally stressed — and *not* 'ku:ltar as the *Oxford Canadian Dictionary* imagines.) In childhood she thought of Canada as part of the great British Empire. Her music took shape in tandem with the growth of Canada's cultural life, population, politics, and ambitions. In her old age, Coulthard knew Canada as a broadly independent cultural force, a nation which in turn honoured her as one of its pre-eminent creative citizens.

Coulthard remained a patriotic, consciously Canadian artist, with an abiding love of French and British culture. As a child she saw Sir Wilfrid Laurier, a great Canadian prime minister. She could recall the reign of King Edward VII, and witnessed the visit of King George VI and the Queen to Canada in 1939. She heard her parents discuss American presidents Wilson, Coolidge, Harding, F.D. Roosevelt, and lived through the governments of Canadian Prime Ministers Wilfrid Laurier, Robert Borden, R.B. Bennett, Mackenzie King, Louis St. Laurent, Diefenbaker, Pearson, and Trudeau.

When she died, in her ninety-third year, the Canadian Prime Minister was Jean Chrétien, and Queen Elizabeth II, whose coronation she celebrated in music with *Prayer for Elizabeth,* had been on the throne for almost fifty years. Coulthard had seen a century of world wars, economic upheaval, and rapid social development. Her life helps us to see how art, music, and an important segment of Canadian society evolved in the twentieth century. To the end, she relied on her West Coast roots, taking artistic nourishment from the ocean, the mountains, and the forests of British Columbia.

Coulthard was a participant in the world of Canadian art music continuously from the 1920s until her death. She saw it all with a keen artist's eye, now and again gently sceptical, but always committed to the Canadian nation and to her beloved British Columbia.

Coulthard visited and worked with great European composers, and enjoyed the good fortune of teaching students who became life-long friends, even when they scattered across the globe. As early as the late 1930s, Jean Coulthard's music was a feature of radio broadcasts in Canada, and then in the United States and Europe. Today a wide selection of her works is available in print and on CD. Generations of students in Canada's conservatories and studios have learned her piano music, played her works for strings, and performed her vocal and choral music. Orchestras and soloists regularly program her larger works.

Her reputation has grown among students of Canadian music, especially with the recent surge of interest in women composers. There are articles on Coulthard in Canada's own music dictionary, *The Encyclopaedia of Music in Canada.* For international perspectives on her work, one can turn to the *New Grove Dictionary of Music and Musicians* or the German musicological dictionary *Die Musik in Geschichte und Gegenwart.*

Jean Coulthard: A Life in Music offers one way of viewing Jean Coulthard's life and music — through words, photographs, and musical examples. We take into account her vision of art, community, politics, and life. But the book is neither in-depth biography nor intensive theoretical analysis. Rather, the authors hope to introduce something of the person and musician that Jean Coulthard was. We hope to reach general readers and listeners, and the many students who might be studying her life or learning her music for performances or examinations. We have incorporated samples from Coulthard's manuscripts, brief analyses of work from each phase of her life, a chronology that connects Coulthard's life to her musical and social contexts, and a selective list of important works from her mammoth catalogue. We include a guide to published and unpublished sources and a discography of currently available CDs.

ACKNOWLEDGEMENTS

THE AUTHORS ARE pleased to recognize the generous assistance of Chris Hives and Erwin Wodarsky of the University of British Columbia Archives, and of UBC Music Librarian Kirsten Walsh and past Music Librarian Hans Burndorfer. We should like also to acknowledge the Canadian Music Centre, its Centredisks program, and CMC-BC's regional director, Colin Miles.

Various other libraries and archive collections have helped in our understanding of Coulthard: CBC Archives, Toronto; Music Division, National Library of Canada, Ottawa; Archives of the City of Vancouver; the Archives of the Royal College of Music, London, UK and the assistant archivist, Peter Gordon; the Librarians and Archivist of the Juilliard School of Music, Lincoln Centre, New York City, New York, USA; the Archives of the Presbyterian Church in America, Philadelphia, Pennsylvania, USA; the Banff Centre, Banff, Alberta.

Among the institutions and associations on which we depended for research assistance and archival documentation were the Conseil municipal de Roquebrune, et son Comité des musées, archives, et centres de culture, Département des Alpes-Maritimes; the Center for the Study of Biography, University of Hawaii, Manoa; and the Research Network for the History of Women in the Professions in Canada, Ontario Institute for Studies in Education, Toronto, Canada.

Many individuals have assisted in the project, among them Mary Gardiner, Frances Balodis, and Elaine Keillor, who read early versions of the manuscript; Gordana Lazarevich; Glenn Colton, Lakehead University; and Professor Jesse Read, School of Music, UBC.

Canada's national broadcaster, the CBC, has long been centrally important in bringing the work of Coulthard to listeners: Karen Wilson; Denise Ball; Harold Gillis; Eitan Cornfield; Don Mowatt; George Laverock; and Peter Togni have shown steadfast support, as has Mario Bernardi, conductor of the CBC Radio Orchestra. We acknowledge Coulthard's major publishers: Novello and Company, Seven Oakes, Kent, UK; Bill Brubacher (Waterloo Music); the Frederick Harris Music Publishing, Ltd.; Ron Napier (Avondale Press); Roberta Stephen (Alberta Keys); and Rick MacMillan of SOCAN.

The authors wish to thank Sylvia Rickard, Jean Ethridge, Chan Ka Nin, Michael Conway Baker, Joan Hansen, Roger Knox, Margaret Bruce, the late Peter Gellhorn, Tom Rolston, Isobel Moore, and the late Violet Archer for invaluable interviews and freely shared documents and photographs.

Russell Wodell has willingly reviewed all sections of the manuscript. His literary and grammatical powers are great, and he has saved us from many errors and sophisms.

Sandra Bruneau has strongly supported this work from beginning to end. Her own activities as musician and writer have shaped our view of Coulthard at every stage of our research and writing.

Coulthard's late sister Babs and the entire Brock family have been generous with information and encouragement. Andreas

Poulsson's photographs have significantly changed the appearance and the meaning of this book, and Jane Adams's documents and recollections, freely given, have made possible the writing of whole sections. Andreas and Janey have our lasting gratitude for their immense contributions.

It is impossible in a work of this size and kind to give a complete, or even a representative list of performers of Jean Coulthard's music. Hundreds, if not thousands of interpreters have made Coulthard's music known over the past sixty-odd years. We hope future scholars will choose to make critical studies of performances of Coulthard's works.

Jean Coulthard loved reading biography, but thought hers was in her *music:* the clues are in the countless texts, themes, and dedications of her compositions. She did not foresee a formal biography, yet gave countless informal interviews, had many informative conversations on drives, and engaged in revealing chats at tea. Ultimately she gave our project her sanction, and the benefit of her lifetime of memories and insight.

ABBREVIATIONS

Complete details for this list of abbreviations, showing the source of each text, appear in the "Complete Citations for Abbreviations," pp. 197–8.

AYIF "A Year in France"
Talk for the Vancouver Women's Musical Club, 1956

CWS "The Cottage on Wiltshire Street"
From *Six Autobiographical Essays,* 1970–1971

DYC "Diary of a Young Composer"
Jean Coulthard. MS journal, 1930–1934

EC "The Eclectic Composer of Today"
Music Magazine, 2, 6 (December 1979): 29

JC/WB Interviews, Jean Coulthard with William Bruneau, 1994–2000
Transcriptions in UBC Archives

JMMC "Jean Coulthard and Canadian Music in the 1930s and 1940s"

MWH "Music is My Whole Life"
Transcription of a talk for Radio Canada International, 1979

PEC "The Pines of Emily Carr"
From *Six Autobiographical Essays,* 1970–1971

THYC "Take Heart, Young Composer!"
Scripted talk: "This Week," CBC Vancouver, 1954

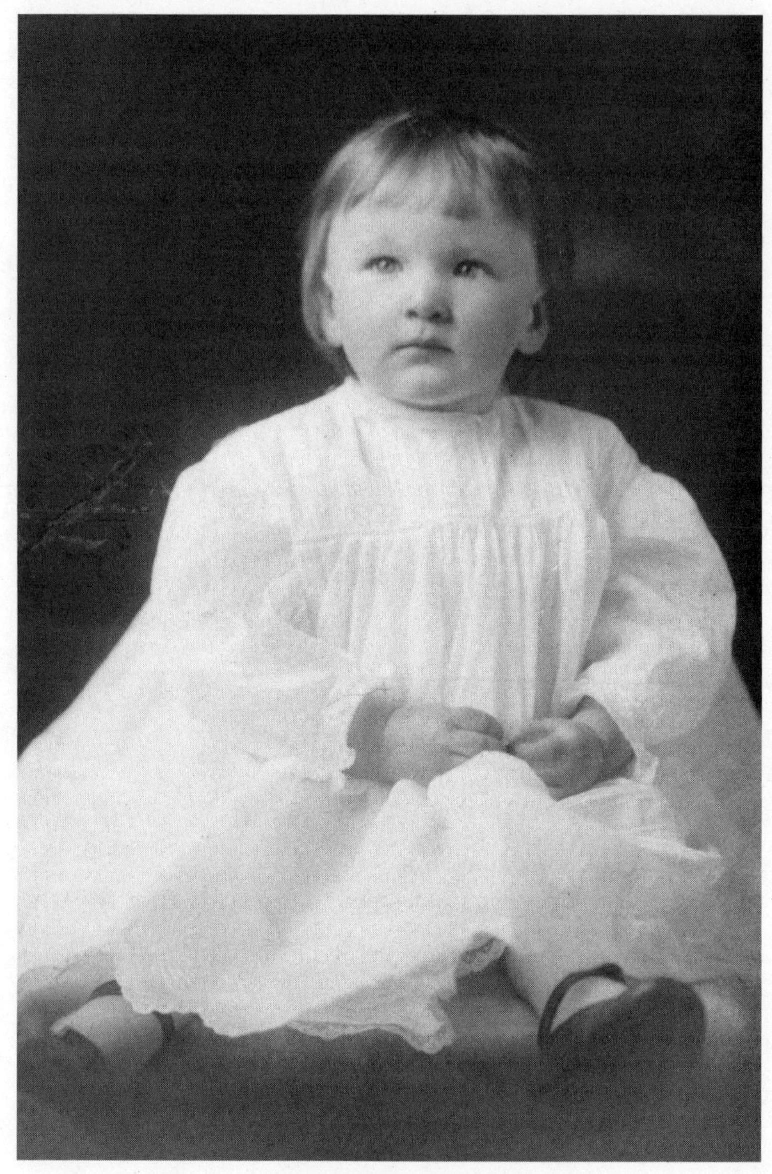

Miss Jean Coulthard

1

A MUSICAL FAMILY

Composer Jean Coulthard spent her last birthday on the tenth of February 2000. Celebrations were subdued. Two years earlier there had been concerts, awards, a huge UBC birthday party, and special family events on the day. But in 2000 there was nothing public, although her spacious apartment (or "flat," as she invariably called it, in the British manner) brimmed with cards and messages from family and friends.

There were flowers for a Coulthard birthday: bouquets of roses and white tulips, potted azaleas, fragrant hyacinths. And always what the English poet and gardener Vita Sackville-West called a "tussie-mussie" of snowdrops, one of the first confirmations of Vancouver's early spring.

Coulthard could look back with satisfaction at a long, productive, and essentially happy life, more than a modicum of fame, the

On the 10th day of Febuary
In the year 1908 A.D.
At 5.10 o'clock in the morning
CAME OUR BABY.
WEIGHING
POUNDS 8 OUNCES 4

Jean Coulthard's baby book

affectionate support of a large, influential circle of professional colleagues, and most significantly, a loving family.

She had been born ninety-two years earlier on a wet, dark morning in pioneer Vancouver. She came into the world at home, on the tenth of February 1908, in Vancouver's residential West End. By then, British Columbia had been in the Canadian confederation for just thirty-seven years, and the transcontinental railway was little more than twenty years old.

Jean was the first child of Dr. and Mrs. Walter Coulthard (née Jean Blake Robinson). Her sister, Margaret (Babs), followed three years later in 1911. The Coulthards were deeply rooted in an Upper Canadian sensibility. Their family particularly valued formal education. Both Coulthard grandfathers held university degrees — a rare thing in Canada before the 1960s — and both were Presbyterian ministers. Grandfather Robinson enjoyed a successful preaching career in Ontario and Quebec, then in the United States before retirement in Manhattan in the mid-1930s. Grandfather

Vancouver, 1911
Vancouver Public Library, VPL 5207 (Photo: Philip Timms)

Coulthard ministered in Ontario nearly all his adult life. Their children, Jean Coulthard's parents, uncles, and aunts — a dozen or so people in the close family grouping — were all professionals or in professional families. Jean's mother graduated with a musical diploma from the New England Conservatory, and her father was a graduate of the University of Toronto.

In the photographic evidence of Jean Coulthard's life, we see the much-loved child of an affluent, colonial Edwardian family. In old age, Coulthard confirmed this view:

> My earliest recollections are being pushed in a little buggy for a walk in the park or to one of the English Bay beaches. My pusher was a Scottish nurse well starched into a white cap and large apron. There were no casually dressed children of professional classes in those days! I remember the borders of large trees and blue-grey sea, like rustling silk. (EC)

Another early recollection was of a sunny Vancouver, in the spring of 1911. The family still lived in a pleasant three-storey house on Broughton Street, complete with picket fence and large gardens front and back. (By 1940, that first Coulthard house was gone, replaced by a small apartment complex — and then, by 2005, enormous highrise buildings.) Photographs of the city in 1911 suggest a

"My pusher was a Scottish nurse"

smoky, sooty place. But that was not Jean Coulthard's recollection of it. Hers was a golden memory of childhood, of sunshine and flowers. For her the city was a clean and an easy place in which to play and grow, with trees, ocean, flowers, and music the constant companions of everyday life.

On this particular day of 1911, the flowers in question were a fine crop of early-March daffodils in a neighbour's front yard. There were three rows of them, thick and beckoning. Eighty-odd years later, Coulthard recalled how in a moment, she — as a tiny girl — had gone to work "harvesting" an entire row of flowers. She took whole plants, and always remembered their look under the bright Vancouver sun. Her arms were full and she could barely stagger under the load of yellow and green.

Her mother came out the door just in time to meet little Jean, complete with daffodils. The grown-up Coulthard's memory was of her mother's beloved face going from delight, to surprise, to horror. The maid, the mother, and the little girl contemplated the empty row on the neighbour's property. In a mother-daughter relation as close and untroubled as this, the momentary clouds on Mrs. Coulthard's face were enough to shock Jean into remembering, forever, her "mistake." She would tell the story of the daffodils all her adult life, always making the same point: "Really, the neighbours should have expected to share those pretty things!"

Family meant, as it does for most children, a whole world of habit, culture, and shared understandings. Her family culture meant that Jean Coulthard's musical efforts received early and strong support. Family culture accounts for the protective insulation that kept young Jean from the harsher aspects of life at the nation's western edge. It also helps to explain how and why a young woman with Jean Coulthard's gifts would choose the demanding life of music and musical composition. Among the Coulthards, self-discipline went back many generations.

Jean's father was as enthusiastic about literature, sculpture, the natural world, and the "art of living" as he was about his profession and his family. He gave music all the support he could at home, and helped keep it alive and well in Vancouver. A coastal man by choice, he enjoyed long sails and Gulf Island vacations, often quoting poets "at the drop of a hat." He and his family spent happy summers at a hotel on Quadra Island, between the British Columbia mainland and Vancouver Island. Dr. Coulthard loved his work, loved nature, and loved the arts.

In particular, he loved music. It was *the* building-block of family life. As Jean Coulthard put it:

Dr. Coulthard and his daughters

> My father was absolutely mad about music. He just loved it and, of course, he loved mother. She played so beautifully in those days; she could sing and do anything and everything in music. We used to play popular songs at Christmas time, but our life was really more serious music. (JC/WB 15 December 1993)

In the days before radio networks and widespread commercial recordings, well-off families spent much time around the piano, and their children learned at least a little about musical notation. It was a skill that would prove essential for the young Jean Coulthard and her career as a composer. In Vancouver, as in most good-sized towns across Canada and the United States, there were piano and violin makers, publishers of sheet music, energetic impresarios, and dozens of music teachers. Even so, the Coulthard family was unusual in its sustained commitment to education in general, and to music in particular.

Vancouver was, after all, an instant city surrounded by ocean and mountains, many hours by boat or train from other Canadian settlements. It was a frontier settlement devoted to transportation and rapacious commerce — there were more saloons than churches. Since its "Great Fire" of 1886, the city had doubled and redoubled in size every five years. The West End remained the genteel corner of Vancouver until 1909, when prosperous families turned their attention to a new development called Shaughnessy Heights. Joining the fashionable migration, Dr. Coulthard moved his family in 1913 to the northern edges of this exclusive instant neighbourhood, having spent just eight years in the West End.

Residents of Shaughnessy no doubt thought themselves more attuned to the arts than other Vancouver residents, and were disproportionately represented at the "better class" of cultural events. Of Vancouver's 120,000 citizens in 1911, about 2,000 regularly attended concerts, and perhaps another 2,000 regularly took part in church music or in popular music activities. The Coulthard family was thus part of a tiny but influential fragment of city society.

Jean and Babs's shared childhood was, by all their accounts, happy. When almost seventy, Coulthard evoked her childhood in

The Coulthards' new house in Shaughnessy

two movements of her orchestral suite *Canada Mosaic* — "Lullaby for a Snowy Night" and "The Contented House." Both girls could read before they entered Cecil Rhodes Public Elementary School, and their progress thereafter was mostly uncomplicated. An inspector said of Jean at the end of Grade I:

> *Summer term. 1914.*
> Reading. Good. Has got on very well.
> Writing. Very good. Most careful and painstaking.
> Arithmetic. Fair. It takes Jean a long time to get hold of things sometimes, but then they stay for good. . . .

Jean believed she had been an introspective and shy child, although by adolescence, she appeared more self-confident. But her recollections of school were not especially rosy, and show that Coulthard's youth was in some respects a "mixed" experience:

> I remember a Mrs. [E.E.] Fletcher. I never could do maths. It was about my second grade, and Mrs. Fletcher was rather an elderly woman. I did something wrong in class, so she decided she'd give me the strap. I had to go to the front of the class and put my hand out. I burst into tears, I was so ashamed. I think it was the most dreadful moment in my whole life for years. (JC/WB, 15 December 1994)

School was necessary and possibly even a good thing, yet contributed little to the creative life of a would-be composer. As children of a music teacher, Jean and Babs began to play the piano before they went to school, as a matter of course. Mother was the arbiter of the girls' musical education and their first music teacher. Even she must have been a trifle surprised when one of her daughters showed a precocious bent for composition.

> All I can remember is that I was at the age where I just loved stories about fairies, so I must have been quite young. I wrote quite a few little pieces. It was Mother made me write them down. She said she would overlook [that] I hadn't had any theory or anything like that. She would help me make the treble clefs and things, but I soon cottoned on. (JC/WB 24 April 1995)

To the non-musician, composing seems an exotic activity. Coulthard was often asked why she chose to become a composer. She developed a pat response.

> I've always been asked how I became a composer. I never consciously decided to *become* one; I think I always *was* one. At the age of seven or eight, I used to compose little pieces at the piano, all about family events. As a child, I was greatly affected by nature too. Perhaps this is why in later life I've used so many nature titles in my music. (MWH)

In April 1919, just after the Great War, Coulthard had her first publication. The popular teachers' magazine *The Educator of Canada* printed a short article called "The Meaning of Rhythm: Little Jean Coulthard Composes Charming Melody." The anonymous author of this item was probably Harry Charlesworth, himself an amateur musician and president of the British Columbia Teachers Federation.

> [A] maiden of nine summers composed the melody and the accompaniment at the request of her teacher [Miss Currie, 9th division, Cecil Rhodes School — now L'Ecole Bilingue] who, needless to say, taught the song to the class, with which it was a general favourite, for they felt it was their 'really' own.[1]

An early Coulthard score, 1917

Coulthard's childhood generally conformed to Edwardian norms, modified by her social class and by Vancouver's colonial environment. She played with neighbourhood children in her father's garden, swam and picnicked in summers, explored the rich coastal scenery on friends' boats and in their newfangled automobiles. By every account, the Coulthards were a cohesive family unit, reasonably well-off in economic terms, healthy and happy.

The adolescent Coulthard would grow to be taller than most of her contemporaries at 5'7½" and the lucky possessor of an oval face framed by light brown hair. She soon acquired the poise to carry out the social obligations of an elder daughter in a professional family, like them or not. By age fifteen, Coulthard's Diary shows that garden parties and long-distance travel no longer worried her, where they sometimes had in earlier childhood.

Her mother recognized and encouraged her daughter's talent and, as a trained professional and music educator, knew how to develop it. Besides, "improvement" was a Presbyterian family's byword, whether or not this particular family saw ahead to the stature their young charge would acquire.

Coulthard's personal ambition and her educational opportunities help to explain how she became a composer, but do not give the complete picture of her taste and aesthetic orientation, which owed much to her mother. Mrs. Walter Coulthard was a well-trained, sophisticated musician in her own right. In 1902–1903 she had spent a year in Boston at the New England Conservatory, and enjoyed renewed contact with the developed music world of Boston and New York during her 1905–1906 honeymoon. She knew her musical classics well, but specialized in modern French music: Debussy, Fauré, Cécile Chaminade, Franck, d'Indy, and even Ravel. This emphasis was unexpected, given the raffish reputation of all things French at the turn of the century. But the music of the early French modernists was to prove a life-long source of delight and inspiration to young Jean Coulthard.

Debussy in particular was her first and strongest influence. The range of colour in his pianistic and orchestral effects, his subtle and flexible sense of rhythm, and his untraditional sonorities formed a musical mother tongue for Coulthard. Together they became the central foundation of her subsequent musical language. But there were others:

> Everyone, I think, feels the musical influences around them at the student stage. I remember my first hero gods were Debussy, Ravel, and Vaughan Williams. And what gods they were to inspire me! As well, my mother gave me a strong classical and romantic background augmented by the contemporary composers of that time, particularly Stravinsky, Debussy, and the French Six. (MWL)

Mrs. Coulthard was about the only figure in Vancouver (perhaps one of the few in Canada) who understood the importance of the French modern masters. In Vancouver, the "West beyond the West," it was not easy to keep abreast of new musical trends.

Even today Vancouverites wishing to feel part of the broad world of the arts must travel. Vancouver is 4,000 kilometres from New York, 2,000 kilometres from Los Angeles, 9,000 kilometres from Paris. Vancouver's pioneers understood travel as a matter of course. To keep up family ties meant lengthy train travel "back East" or sea voyages to Europe.

What gave Mrs. Coulthard's travels a peculiar distinction was their educational and musical purposes. Mrs. Coulthard intended to further musical life in Vancouver, and to make it a viable musical centre. She needed to know more, much more about music and music education.

As one of the few well-trained voice teachers in western Canada, Mrs. Coulthard parlayed her training and her professional reputation into a lucrative business: a professionally run music teaching studio. To survive, the owner of a music studio in rough and tumble Vancouver had to be "famous." In order to be famous, and to be knowledgeable, one had to travel and to be known to have travelled. It is hard be a prophet in one's own country, but for a Canadian it is very hard.

In the winter of 1918–1919, she felt the need of a refresher trip to Boston and New York. She spent it studying advanced voice production and breathing technique at the New England Conservatory of Music in Boston, and with a private coach in New York City. Jean and Babs stayed with their Robinson grandparents in Wellsburg, West Virginia, attending an American public school for the year. Mrs. Coulthard rode the trains to and from month-long sessions.

Jean retained precise memories of her travel. It was expensive and difficult. Trains were drawn by great steam engines, fed by coal from mines across the land. Passengers might be covered in cinders at any time.

> Mummy used to take us East. We would visit Ontario, Quebec, and New Brunswick every two to three years. It was always by train. We'd have special things made to go on the train. We had dark silk dresses, because the soot used to come in the windows and get all over you! (JC/WB, 15 December 1993)

Mrs. Coulthard spent hours combing cinders out of her daughters' hair. In winter, train travel required the stoking of little furnaces in each passenger car to prevent frostbite.

Jean, her mother, and Babs in the studio, 1511 Marpole Street

Once, in deep winter, the CPR train pulled into a station in late afternoon. It was cold and sunny, and the girls asked to be allowed to run up and down the station platform, but Mrs. Coulthard — by now a partisan Vancouverite — declared: "Pull down the shades, children, it's *Winnipeg!*" (JC/WB 25 January 1996)

The travel turned out to be well worth the trouble and the cost. Mrs. Coulthard became something of a local arts celebrity, with a long record of solo work in the Christ Church Cathedral Choir in such popular classical works as Handel's *Messiah,* Mendelssohn's *Elijah,* and Haydn's *Creation,* and occasional benefit recitals of solo works under church auspices. Whenever Mrs. Coulthard performed, the daily papers mentioned the fact with appropriately positive, even gushing praise. All too few Canadians possessed the knowledge and the art to do what Mrs. Coulthard could, and the newspapers found her work worthy of dozens of column inches. Mrs. Coulthard made sure the press knew about her performances, but also the the recitals of her pupils — and insisted reporters attend in person. Until the abrupt end of her life, the *Vancouver Province* and the *News Advertiser* would offer photographs of and interviews with "the gracious lady of Vancouver music."

In her efforts to give Vancouver a vital musical life, Mrs. Coulthard corralled any of the steady stream of "important" musical visitors who passed through the city, persuading them to give recitals, lectures, and even master classes. In some cases Mrs. Coulthard acted as impresario, in others she took advantage of musical visitors on tours organized by others. The early visits of the Cherniavsky Trio (who will return to this story in a moment) were organized by a San Francisco impresario, but once the Trio was known to be coming to Vancouver, Mrs. Coulthard quickly found a way to make use of these three artists — in this case, to give special lessons for a day or two to her best pupils, and to other music students of her acquaintance. Vancouver might be isolated in its north-west, North-American fastness, but it was also a resting place in the transportation system linking the Canadian east, the western United States, and Asian outposts of the old Empire. The musical "great and good" had to pass through Vancouver.

Mrs. Walter Coulthard: "The gracious lady of Vancouver music"

Mrs. Coulthard's success in attracting violinists, singers, and pianists to Vancouver impressed her young daughter:

> One of mother's endeavours was to organize the Vancouver Women's Musical Club. In those days, one must remember, there were many concert tours by fine artists. My mother and her group of enthusiasts were ambitious enough to bring such people as Walter Damrosch, Anna Pavlova, and Madame Gadski to the Vancouver scene. Sometimes they got into real jams over the financial part of it. But nothing daunted; they were artful and clever enough to see their way out of it with gifts from interested donors! (MWL)

Mrs. Coulthard's public mission contributed to a private one. She ran the largest piano-and-voice-teaching studio in town. Under her guidance, her daughters embraced the practical discipline of trained performing musicians: intense and regularly-scheduled lessons, competitions, examinations, public recitals, and countless hours of practice. Nobody in the family was sure if Jean or Babs would enter the tough world of competitive performance, but both girls were in any case prepared.

> Babs had the most wonderful voice when she was just a young girl of 18. She could sing up to a high C without any trouble at all — a really lovely, lovely voice. She was a very pretty young woman. And Mother put her in the Bach festivals that used to be held here, and the adjudicators said that she had the perfect sound in her voice for singing Bach, and that if she continued she would make one of the world's Bach singers. And of course Mother was simply thrilled at this. (JC/WB, 10 December 1997)

The moment Jean Coulthard was old enough (just before her seventeenth birthday) she joined her mother in teaching, as did Babs when *her* seventeenth birthday came. In Jean's case, the year was 1925. That fall, with her parents' encouragement, she decided to attend Arts courses at the University of British Columbia. She stuck with her courses until Christmas, when it was plain that her music teaching, private musical studies, and compositional goals were simply inconsistent with the full-time demands of a B.A. degree in literature. Jean dropped out at Christmas without regret, giving herself fully to musical life, teaching in the Coulthard studio, and of course continuing her own musical study and practice. By this time, the daughters saw their place in their mother's well-honed promotional strategy. Jean certainly recognized her mother's executive role as founder of the family enterprise, and accepted her own and her sister's roles in it.

Jean saw that she would contribute piano and theory teaching to the business. Babs would follow in her mother's footsteps as a singer. In her *Vancouver Province* advertisements, Mrs. Coulthard promised her pupils a strong basis "in every aspect of musical art and production."[2] The Coulthard women delivered.

In her teens, Jean had begun studies with Frederick Chubb,[3] organist at Christ Church Cathedral from 1912 through World War II. Chubb came to Vancouver with degrees and diplomas from Oxford and Cambridge, and a deep well of knowledge about English cathedral music. He knew his music theory backwards and forwards. Jean always acknowledged what she learned from him:

> When I began serious lessons in theory, my first real teacher was Frederick Chubb, the British-trained organist of Ely Cathedral [by then of Vancouver's Christ Church Cathedral]. I was about seventeen and he was a remarkably musical and imaginative man. (MWL)

With Chubb teaching her theory, and Mrs. Coulthard piano, Jean began intermittent work toward a diploma from the Toronto Conservatory, and her piano playing progressed toward professional levels. Serious pianists come to know the long, lonely hours of practice, discipline, and commitment needed for concert work. It was a lesson Coulthard would apply throughout her life as a composer.

Despite Frederick Chubb's technical expertise and the Coulthard family's commitment to music, Vancouver lacked the musical infrastructure to motivate Coulthard. The city's tastes were hopelessly provincial:

> When we heard Ravel in 1928 it must have been in the horrible old Georgia Auditorium (which is fortunately no longer in use), a cavernous arena-like space with very poor sound. Ravel was very slim and small, rather delicate-looking. He played almost like a young child — very simple and no 'concert pianist' style at all. One piece I remember in particular was the *Pavane;* he played it very simply with almost no expression at all. . . . All this certainly did not appeal to the Vancouver audience, who knew little or nothing about Ravel. They were here to hear a "real concert pianist" plus a virtuoso singer. True, there was a small and very appreciative group present but, to the great embarrassment of my mother and other musicians in her circle like Frederick Chubb and Mrs. Della Johnson, the audience started going out in droves after the first couple of numbers. By the end of the concert there were fewer than fifty left. . . . My mother took great pains to explain to my sister and me that Ravel was not a virtuoso but a *great* composer.[4]

For a developing young composer, it was time to move on — if she could find a way to do so.

The Vancouver Women's Musical Club instituted a scholarship in 1926, and began holding recitals, teas, and bric-a-brac sales to raise money for it. A scholarship winner was expected to study in England. By 1928 the scholarship was funded and open to competition. Jean applied, learning in early June she had won the scholarship, and excitedly prepared to leave for a year's study at the Royal College of Music.

London was the political and cultural centre of the Empire. Royal College of Music examiners went out to the larger Canadian cities to test musicians for associateship, licentiateship, and fellowship in the diplomas of the Associated Schools of Music of London. Mr. Chubb had encouraged the young Jean to think of sitting for a Licentiate from the Schools. What better way to begin than a whole *year* in London, studying at the very source?

Under most circumstances the Coulthards would not have considered sending their provincial twenty-year-old daughter to a world capital on her own. Conveniently, Jean's father's brother Howard

En route to England

The Royal College of Music

Coulthard had retired to England after a successful career as a doctor on the Canadian Pacific Steam Ship Lines. Over the years Jean had enjoyed "occasional visits" from her uncle when he served as a medical doctor on the *Empress of Japan,* a luxury ship that plied back and forth to the Orient. Jean recalled that "he would bring us Chinese dolls and fine silks for my Mother's wardrobe." (EC)

After his retirement from the CPR, Uncle Howard and his long-time friend Captain Ernest Haskett-Smith bought a large Victorian-style home in Roehampton, then a suburb of London, about a forty-five-minute bus ride from the Royal College of Music. He was good to his niece. Jean remembered that he

> . . . rented a beautiful grand piano for me and kept it in the living room so I could practice comfortably. He had two servants, Annie and Eva, who had their own apartment beautifully fixed in the basement. It was very much like *Upstairs Downstairs.* They were delighted to have a young girl in the house, and spoiled me. I wasn't fit to live with. Mother was furious with me when I came home! (JC/WB, 24 April 1995)

A provincial Cinderella with "the uncles," Coulthard was to have an exhilarating taste of the great world beyond Vancouver. She confessed to being "spoiled rotten" with two maids and "lots of concerts, and trips here and there." She recalled a performance of Samuel Coleridge-Taylor's popular oratorio *Hiawatha* in which, at a particularly dramatic moment, artificial snow fell from high up in the roof of the massive Royal Albert Hall.

Coulthard went to London a shy provincial, even younger than her years suggest. As contemporary pictures show, her year in London transformed her into a facsimile of a sophisticated young woman of the world, smartly clothed in the best and newest style, complete with affected walking stick (in old age, looking over seventy-year-old photographs, Coulthard added the sarcastic caption on the back of one portrait: "Funny child!").

She made friends in London with young people from all over Britain and the Empire. In April 1929 she accompanied her new friend Australian pianist Ruth Pasco and other College students on a spring tour of Germany.[5] In Cologne she heard one of the first performances of avant-garde composer Paul Hindemith's opera *Cardillac,* about a goldsmith who murders his clients to steal back the jewellery he has made for them. Coulthard admired the music — but also the "fine young British navy boys then stationed on the Rhine. We *did* have fun, you know."

Coulthard's teachers at the Royal College of Music included Kathleen Long, an internationally renowned London piano per-

"Funny child"

former and teacher, and R.O. Morris, who taught her all about fugues and canons.

> I did practise quite religiously, though not in the early part of my English stay, as I was busy seeing London. The uncles had tickets for everything, of course. Kathleen Long knew I was just there for the year, so she had no particular plan for me. I worked up the Beethoven *Sonata* no. 15, a lovely one, and Bach's *Chromatic Fantasy and Fugue.* Oh, I had a stiff program. When I came home I kept on practising it another year with Mother's help, and then had my

Dearest Grands: How do you like this! We are having a wonderful trip.. this is taken half way up the Drachenfel mountain on the bank of the Rhine: We had such fun as we climbed up the mountain on these sweet donkeys. mine was called Hanz! I laughed the whole way up. till I was almost ill! The other girl is Ruth Pasco who is travelling with me - & the boy is another London student whom we met in Cologne. At the top of the mountain are the ruins of an old castle built in 1100! Simply beautiful! We passed through Bonn & saw Beethovens birth place - Love Jeannie

A postcard from Germany, 1929 (Jean on left)

> debut in Vancouver — for the IODE [Imperial Order of the Daughters of the Empire] chapter, a big thing in those days. (JC/WB, 24 April 1995)

In October 1928 Coulthard had a second glimpse of Maurice Ravel when he visited London and the Royal College — wearing a purple velvet morning coat — to perform and lecture. The College hall was filled to the rafters, and this time nobody thought of early departure.

For composition lessons, the College Registrar assigned her to Ralph Vaughan Williams, then England's most important modern composer and at the height of his powers. Earlier he had championed folk music and the rediscovery of the pre-baroque English masters. But he was no teacher, and Coulthard was young and timid.

> There was never time for Vaughan Williams to do any of his compositions over with me: Half an hour and my time was up! I was too young to insist. The thought never seemed to have entered my head to bring one of his symphonies without first asking. I cannot remember if I was plain stupid or too young, or whether Vaughan Williams had no idea how to tackle a pupil in an orthodox manner. (DYC, 23 January 1931)

Coulthard was always proud to have studied with Vaughan Williams, but came to realize he was a rather uninspired composition teacher. Although Vaughan Williams would suggest little writing exercises or analysis projects, there was no system in his approach, and it was difficult for Coulthard to progress or to learn.

> I never felt the thrill of inspiration at his lessons. . . . I can't honestly say that Vaughan Williams gave me one thought to brood on or bite on. I felt so homesick, miserable, and squashed. . . . One day, he remarked on the pretty clothes I wore, and said how sweet of me to cheer up an old man in a dingy college room. I remember wishing fervently my music had called for a few remarks instead of my spring frock! (DYC, entry for 23 January 1931)

At all events, living and learning in London shaped Coulthard's world-view. Kensington Gardens, the Victoria and Albert Museum,

Ralph Vaughan Williams

the Royal Albert Hall, the Natural History Museum (to say nothing of the smart shops) were within easy distance, and the musical exposure extended her general education. She heard first-rate performances and felt herself a tiny part of grand traditions in art and music.

Long afterward, she understood she had missed opportunities at the College. She readily admitted that she might have practised piano much harder than she did; and if her aim had been to

Jean as a debutante, 1927

become a "real composer," then her time had been largely squandered. It would take years to correct that weak beginning. In the summer of 1929, however, it was almost time to return to the West Coast of Canada.

Mrs. Coulthard had written her daughter once- or even twice-weekly all through 1928–1929, and had crossed the Atlantic at the beginning of Jean's stay in London, and then at the end. To celebrate the finish of the school year, Mother organized a special two-week-long holiday in Paris. It began with a clothes-buying spree in London, featuring a Burberry coat subsidized by the beneficent Uncle Howard, and a set of Scottish sweaters found in a Kensington shop.

Then it was on to France. As always, August in Paris was hot and, for a young woman of twenty-one, terribly exciting. Uncle Ernest, who knew Paris well, arranged a detailed program of "museum-hunts" and visits in the Paris region. In early September it was all over. Mother, daughter, uncle, and a friend took the Channel Train from the Gare du Nord, on to Calais, then to Southampton. With that, a change of ships, and the Coulthards, mother and daughter, headed home to Canada.

> I wept like a girl in 1928, leaving my family behind — and then in 1929 wept all the way home, leaving London . . . forever? Gradually I got over England, although I moped for a long time. I must have been the most horrible child when I came home. Mercifully, Mother needed me in the junior studio, to take the junior students. Babs was too young then, being three years younger, to do the teaching. I pitched in. I think it was fate that I should come home. There was so little time to have with Mother. . . . (JC/WB, 24 April 1995)

This time on a French liner, the Coulthards found themselves mid-ship in an inside cabin, and in the care of a pair of Norman chambermaids. The weather was dreadful, the food surprisingly bad, and one day out of Montreal, as the Coulthards' luggage was opened for inspection, all their fine Scottish sweaters could no longer be found. Indeed, a quarter of Jean Coulthard's worldly goods had vanished. A company agent, "l'inspecteur," could make no headway, and the Norman chambermaids were suddenly mute. For a young artist, it must have seemed a strange end to a year in Europe. As it turned out, Jean Coulthard would not see England again for exactly twenty years.

Jean Coulthard by John Vanderpant

2

MUSIC IN HARD TIMES

Soon after Jean Coulthard returned to Vancouver in September 1929, times became very hard. The Fascists had taken power in Italy and the Nazis would soon rule Germany. After a long boom, the North American economy moved toward collapse. Canada faced severe financial crises.

In Vancouver in 1930, nearly ten thousand men applied for financial aid to keep their families from starvation. That number tripled by the mid-1930s. The City of Vancouver teetered at the edge of bankruptcy all through 1935 and 1936. It saw violent skirmishes as crowds of unemployed — some of whom had ridden the rails across the country — confronted the authorities in the Post Office riot of 1935.

All around the city, unemployed and destitute people looked for help, and too often did not receive it. Even at 1511 Marpole Street, the social turmoil had resonances. Two days before Hallowe'en

1931, at 4 a.m., the Coulthard daughters woke up to the sound of breaking glass. Jean and Babs tiptoed to the upstairs hall-door, peered out, and could just make out the heavy (and muddy) boots of a large person making a quick exit. The girls woke Dr. Coulthard, giving him a huge broom for purposes of self-defence. By the time Dr. Coulthard arrived to deal with the intruder, the man was long gone. It was a failed burglary, a sign of the social distress already well-rooted in Depression-era Vancouver.

The Coulthard family developed its own problems. Dr. Coulthard had been steadily losing his hearing. The family reorganized to adapt to his disability. As he grew more and more deaf, and had fewer patients, the importance of the music studio increased.

In tough times, the arts are often considered something that can be painlessly cut from civic and family budgets. Students began dropping out of the Coulthard studio. Mrs. Coulthard still managed to combine lofty ideas of art and culture with the hardheaded business instincts of a natural businesswoman. Using her social connections, she effectively promoted her activities as performer and teacher. Jean and Babs lived lives outsiders might have considered privileged. For all anyone knew, these were well-off young ladies of their class. Coulthard's daily life was a round of playing, teaching, and socializing.

Like many young people, she kept a diary. To help keep its contents from prying eyes, she wrote her occasional entries on the last hundred-odd pages of her notebook on orchestration, "Hiding behind the orchestral notes in the front of this book. Hiding behind the percussion."[6] The document never once mentions the difficulties most Vancouver people had in everyday life. Although Coulthard would soon learn how difficult life could be, Jean and Babs had been carefully insulated by their protective parents. Her *Diary* offers an almost precious depiction of the long post-Edwardian twilight lived by well-off Vancouverites. Clothes, parties, picnics and sailing trips receive the lion's share of the young composer's attention — when not discussing the "finer things," music and poetry. Still, this self-portrait, however self-absorbed, rings true. Even its adolescent pretense is right.

Janey and Peter Cherniavsky in the garden at Shannon

In the early 1930s, the city still resembled frontier boom towns on both sides of the Canadian-American border. Despite the hard times, forms of artistic life continued. Vancouverites knew and loved their vaudeville houses, and new movie palaces like the Orpheum on Granville Street.[7] The Vancouver Symphony was struggling to be born, and the days of regular public recital series were far off. A few wealthy Vancouver families regularly welcomed friends and musicians to teas and private recitals in their homes.

Pre-eminent among them was the salon of Mrs. B.T. Rogers, where Coulthard had entrée. Mrs. Rogers was the wife of an American-born entrepreneur who had established the B.C. Sugar Refinery. She lived in a spectacular neo-Georgian mansion, "Shannon," that occupied several city blocks on the then-southern edge of Vancouver at Granville Street and 57th Avenue. Cultural and social celebrities from far beyond Vancouver turned up for tea with Mrs. Rogers in her large, mirror-filled music room — anyone from the Prince of Wales (later King Edward VIII) to Australia's redoubtable soprano, Nelly Melba. Here Jean Coulthard met Jan Cherniavsky (1892–1989), the internationally known pianist from the Cherniavsky Trio *and* Mrs. Rogers' son-in-law. Mrs. Coulthard

Charcoal sketch, 1943, of Jan Cherniavsky by Myfanwy Spencer Pavelic, with kind permission of Peter Cherniavsky

persuaded him to accept Jean as an occasional piano student. Jan Cherniavsky was thought to be a phenomenon. Merely to know him was an extraordinary experience for the twenty-something Jean Coulthard.

> Jan was a fiery, crazy Russian, there was nothing truer than that . . . I'd play something, and he'd say, *"But it means nothing! It means nothing the way you play it!"* Oh, I used to end up in tears with Jan, lots of times. He was a wonderful master of teaching you how music should really sound. . . . He never bothered to teach technique or anything, he said, *"You do that yourself. You do all that. I want to teach you how music should sound. . . ."* As for my composition, he was no more interested in that — and that was a little bit of a sore spot with me — because I was aiming to be a composer, but he was no more interested in any pieces I wrote than . . . a fly on the wall. (JC/WB 24 April 1995)

Mrs. Coulthard and Cherniavsky worked out a barter arrangement. Jean would take lessons with Jan. Jan's children, Janey and Peter, would come to Jean for their first piano lessons.

Coulthard also continued her theory lessons with Mr. Chubb, with the practical objective of earning diplomas. She found it hard to concentrate on traditional academic theory when she wanted to *compose,* not to study for dry exams in counterpoint and harmony from faraway Toronto and London.

> The results have come, counterpoint passed, harmony failed, and the teachers a kick in the eye! Aside from writing various sets of 5ths, octaves, and leading-up 3rds of chords, jumping from the bass of 6/4 chords, and utterly ignoring dominant 13ths, I did not do as badly as I expected to! However, let us cheerfully shut our eyes, nose, and throat to such unmusical thoughts and begin again. (DYC)

In 1931, Coulthard received the LRAM (Licentiate of the Royal Academy of Music and of the Royal College of Music) in piano and pedagogy. Three years later Coulthard added a second teaching diploma, the ATCM (Associateship of the Toronto Conservatory of Music).

Coulthard was now far more interested in composing than in playing. She regularly produced piano pieces, songs, even an anthem or two — almost all "withdrawn" at later times, although now available in Coulthard's papers. In the 1930s, music composition was outside the scope of most universities. There were few teachers of composition, most of whom taught in time-honoured master-apprenticeship arrangements. In Toronto or Montreal, English curricula — held over from Victorian days — stressed academic set-piece compositions. On the whole, teachers and students of creative composition were rare.

> This morning I had an inspiring lesson with Mr. Chubb. Having written two fugues, I feel weightier. I wonder why! I happen to be the first pupil of Mr. Chubb's who has written two (so he told me). That describes the musical state of Vancouver, B.C., without another word. (DYC)

Although Coulthard's education in piano and theory gave her a good starting point in technical and artistic terms, she had still to make her own way as a composer. Her ambition and drive to compose were strong and resilient.[8]

Then the family's secure foundations were shaken by parental illness. Dr. Coulthard became entirely unable to work.

> My father's deafness was quite a tragedy. His medical practice gradually faded away because you simply had to scream at him finally to make him hear. He ended up doing life insurance examinations and things like that. (JC/WB 14 April 1995)

Of necessity, the three Coulthard women became primary breadwinners as well as music teachers. Few of their genteel Shaughnessy connections realized the quiet desperation of the Coulthard women. On the surface, all was as before. The studio remained a well-organized affair. Perhaps a hundred pupils came and went each week. But it was a business on a knife-edge: if they lost ten pupils, they faced instant and dire consequences.

In late June 1933, a second calamity occurred. Mrs. Coulthard suffered an appendix attack, which went undiagnosed until it had become a severe infection. There were no antibiotics yet. A projected two-day stay in the old Vancouver General Hospital became ten days of increasing agony before Mrs. Coulthard finally died of peritonitis. Jean's and Babs's secure world was forever shattered.

In a postscript to her *Diary of a Young Composer,* Coulthard confides that

> it has been a hard year to pull through. To have to adjust oneself to the absence of one who is our inspiration, comfort, and the light of our house is not easy. Mother was the essence of everything good to me. (DYC)

Coulthard now renewed her acquaintance with a childhood friend, Donald Marvin Adams. Jean and Don had met at a garden party in the 1920s and had stayed in touch. Adams had spent several years in Berkeley, California before returning to Canada in 1934. As he mentioned in a later memoir,

> I was nineteen years of age in 1927 when I went to Berkeley. . . . To a young man such as I, brought up in the rather colonial city of Victoria, where the only creative mind at work was that of Emily Carr — whose broad canvases were the subject of derision and contempt — the university town of Berkeley seemed a world apart. I

Mrs. Coulthard in the 1930s

> became actively involved with architects, designers, painters, composers, musicians, and photographers, who were expressing themselves in new and exciting forms of expression and development.[9]

Among these acquaintances were architect Raymond Yelland (whose Tupper and Reed building is still one of Berkeley's landmarks), arts and crafts master Bernard Maybeck, and photographers Ansel Adams and Edward Weston.

For all anyone knew, Don was just another friend. The *Diary of a Young Composer* tells a different tale. Coulthard had her eye on him and looked forward to his return with a romantic mixture of curiosity, anticipation, and apprehension.

Within eighteen months of her mother's death, Don and Jean were married, on Christmas Eve 1935.

After a week's honeymoon in Seattle, Don and Jean lived in the Coulthard home on Marpole Street for several years. Don took a job selling sheet music. He resented this prosaic employment, but understood he was lucky to have a job. Married life in the Coulthard family home, which came complete with Jean's father and sister, presented moments of difficulty. Then in 1937 her father died — deaf and isolated. The happy home life of Coulthard's childhood had vanished.

At thirty, she acquired the full adult responsibilities of marriage, managing a household, and maintaining a studio. Coulthard became increasingly systematic and practical. There are record books showing her organized approach to students, fees, examinations, and concert performances.

She was also growing as an artist. She began the life-long practice of making sense of her life through her art. Her motto, indeed her *raison d'être:* "Music is my whole life. If one can interpret it, one can understand my personal philosophy." (MWL)

Throughout her career Coulthard would write numerous works named "Threnody" — a lament, derived from the Greek *threnoidia,* from *threnos* (wailing) and *oide* (song). Coulthard's first *Threnody,* a setting of a text by seventeenth-century English poet Robert Herrick, was in memory of "JRC" — her mother.

Threnody

Coulthard knew almost instinctively about the private side of the art of composition. The public, professional role of a composer was another matter. What did it mean to be a Canadian woman in her twenties and thirties who composed?

Composition requires long hours of hard, uninterrupted, and surprisingly dull work — hours that had to be extracted from an already-full life. After Jean Coulthard's death, the only extant evidence of Jean Coulthard-the-cartoonist was discovered buried in her papers: a slightly confused sketch showing a self-caricature of the composer trying to work at the piano with dogs demanding walks, husband demanding dinner, delivery men coming to the door, domestic help requiring supervision, and a tiresome student on the phone — a double fugue of whirling distractions.

Coulthard was learning to balance teaching, composing, and managing a home. She was also beginning to interest other people in performing her music. Only a few years earlier, she had usually been her own best choice as performer. Thus she was pianist in the few known performances of the piano quintet, one such occasion being in Mrs. Rogers's Music Room.

> I performed quite a lot — my repertoire included Stravinsky, Prokofiev, da Falla, Chavez, Medtner — and on occasion I performed my own songs and piano music on the local scene and on radio. Deems Taylor used to talk about new music and composers over the radio during the intermission period of the New York Philharmonic Concerts. One day he announced that a conductor in Reading, Pennsylvania would undertake to play works by new as yet unknown composers providing they were up to a professional standard. Of course I, simply full of ambition, sent off my one and only orchestral score, entitled "Portrait." To my utter amazement it was accepted and played. This piece has long since been withdrawn from my catalogue, needless to say. I had not much understanding of orchestration at that time, and certainly the piece was not up to professional standard. (MWH)

Coulthard was gradually learning to be self-critical. She would sketch and experiment, keep the good bits, and the potential hits, and suppress the rest. Coulthard believed in "inspiration" and knew when she had created something that might be of value. She was lucky with one of her earliest vocal productions, the *Cradle Song* of 1931, and its many later variants. This work was eventually written and rewritten for solo voice, for chorus with accompaniment,

Pianist/composer: 1936 publicity photo

and for voice with small orchestra. Another persuasive example would be her early song *Frolic* (text by Æ, pseudonym for G.W. Russell, a then-popular Irish dramatist and scholar). Coulthard found the poem for this work in the 1930s, and made a first setting in 1934. She included an extensively re-written form of the piece in her 1960s cycle of *Six Irish Poems.*

In this pattern of early compositions, rejected and withdrawn, followed by sober second thoughts, and sometimes by revivals, Coulthard was a typical composer. We are unusually lucky to be able to trace the sequence of composition from early experiments to later successes: the Archives of the University of British Columbia has all the old pieces, neatly written, often covered with personal notations and corrections, sometimes successful and later published or performed, often not.

THE MUSIC: *Variations on Good King Wenceslas* (1934)

Jean Coulthard was just twenty-five years old when she wrote the *Variations on Good King Wenceslas* for solo piano. She often performed this work herself as a party-piece for friends and family at receptions and get-togethers, particularly in the Christmas season.

The theme of this conventional set of variations is the well known carol. Coulthard thought the tune was a thirteenth-century spring carol, but the words — fanciful words at that — were added by Victorian Englishman John Mason Neale in 1853.

Coulthard provided her own harmonization of the tune and then composed a number of variations, each prefaced with a line of text.

THEME: "Good King Wenceslas looked out on the feast of Stephen"

In the first variation the tune moves into the left hand, with sixteenth-note patterns in the right.

VARIATION 1: "Brightly shone the moon that night"

The second variation is a free canon. Both parts present elaborated versions of the original tune.

VARIATION 2: "Page and monarch, forth they went"

The third variation, cast in the tonic minor, is plaintive and chorale-like.

VARIATION 3: "When a poor man came in sight, gath'ring winter fuel"

The final variation (and the moral of the tale) is the most difficult and effective: it is in the style of one of the great chorale preludes of J.S. Bach, and weaves the theme into a set of elaborate sixteenth-note flourishes — a joyous and brilliant conclusion to a delightful set of variations.

VARIATION 4: "Ye who now will help the poor shall yourselves find blessing"

As Coulthard's compositional powers grew in the 1930s, her output increased accordingly. She put away many pieces from her teens and twenties; when she found them in old files, sometimes decades later, she often as not suppressed them altogether, and removed them from her official catalogue. In the 1970s, when she and her students were working on the teaching pieces published as *Music of Our Time,* Coulthard remembered that first set of variations, and over forty years later re-introduced them to young pianists. She did not find unworthy *all* the music she wrote as a young woman.

Mrs. Donald Adams: Jean Coulthard in the mid-1930s

As a performer, Coulthard had direct opportunity to judge her music and its effect on stage. By 1938, she had been invited with Michael Dyne (an English actor/writer en route to Hollywood) to give a series of illustrated recital-lectures on CBR, the local Vancouver station of the Canadian Broadcasting Corporation radio network. The CBC was then just two years old. If the thirty-year-old Coulthard did not yet entirely understand radio's importance for Canadian culture, it at least meant welcome exposure and modest income.

> Ira Dilworth came to take over the newly organized CBC in British Columbia. . . . Somehow or other, by the later 1930s a feeling of change *was* slowly becoming apparent in several ways, and it was then that I realized I was indeed on the ground floor of Canadian music in the West. From then on, it was inspiring. (MWH)

By the end of the 1930s Coulthard aspired to be nothing less than a full-time composer. But industry and commitment, however great, were not enough to make her the sort of artist she intended to be. Her only compositional training thus far — in London — had been not at all practical. Because of his years in California, Don Adams had a better sense of musical developments in the United States.

> Don . . . introduced me to new music developments from the United States perspective. I became acquainted with the work of Copland, Harris, Cowell (whose *New Music* magazine we all read and studied), and even the early fascinating and controversial ideas of John Cage, who lived in Seattle in those years. (JCCM)

Coulthard's first personal experience with a committed modernist composer came when she took her new husband to visit her grandparents in New York. While there she arranged to have a few study lessons with Aaron Copland, only eight years older than Coul-

Aaron Copland

thard but already a successful artist, well aware of the business, political, and promotional sides of a composer's working life. Copland received the young woman from the West Coast graciously.

> I phoned Copland from my grandmother's. He said yes, that he'd be pleased that I come and see him. So I brought my compositions . . . written for my grandmother and grandfather for Christmas, *Variations on Good King Wenceslas.* I played those to him (I used to play quite well in those days). He wasn't very impressed . . . but he was a very kindly man and he gave us tickets to concerts and things that otherwise we wouldn't have been able to go to. (JC/WB 22 January 1994)

The meeting was good for her confidence, but underlined the absolute necessity of acquiring a stronger basis in composition.

The years 1938–1939 were among the most troubling of the twentieth century. War became more likely with each passing month, and many artists in totalitarian lands across the world had simple survival as their most pressing need. World events touched the Coulthard family: Jean Coulthard's sister Babs had just married writer David Brock (1910–1978) and was spending a year abroad in England. Coulthard was more than a little relieved when High Commission officials told Babs and her husband that it was time to return home.

The cultural landscape of the Pacific coast was about to change dramatically. Thousands of Europeans, particularly those who were Jewish or who had left-wing political views, found safe refuge from the dangers of Europe in the western-most regions of North America: Arnold Schoenberg, Igor Stravinsky, Berthold Brecht, Thomas Mann and his well-known brother Heinrich, and dozens more, all moved to the Los Angeles area. Darius Milhaud went to Oakland. And composer and conductor Arthur Benjamin came to Vancouver.

Jean Coulthard joined a tiny circle of composers, Leonard Basham (or Robert Barclay, as he liked to be called) and Robert Fleming among them, who went to Benjamin for lessons. "Benjie" made quite a stir:

Arthur Benjamin

> Benjamin played attractive music in his own symphony series — his Proms — interesting things that the Symphony wouldn't dare to do. They became so popular that the Symphony girls — old Amy Buckerfield (a perfect dear and all the rest) — couldn't *stand* it. They were absolutely death on him because they felt he was taking away from the Symphony and the town wasn't big enough for two. They made it so miserable for him that he simply left after the War. Vancouver lost a great man and a great artist. (JC/WB 12 January 1996)

Although Benjamin's music is not much played today, he was a powerful, established figure with grand plans for his brood of young Canadians. He wanted Coulthard to move beyond songs, piano pieces, and chamber works and to write more for orchestra. It helped that Benjamin could program Coulthard's work — and in short order she experienced the thrill of hearing her work properly rehearsed and presented by a professional orchestra.

Coulthard produced the *Ballade "A Winter's Tale"* for large string orchestra, and British Columbia's first ballet score, *Excursion* (still unstaged). Jean's new brother-in-law, writer, humorist, and future broadcaster David Brock, contributed *Excursion's* bitter-sweet scenario of love in wartime, set in British Columbia's Gulf Islands.

Jean and Don now lived on their own in a modest house in the streetcar suburb of Kerrisdale.

> It was a cottage-type house built of white clapboards and gable roofs hidden at the back of a pretty garden of tall trees and herbaceous borders. It was Love-in-a-Cottage also, for there were never two happier people. (CWS)

In 1939 World War II began. Today we remember the "real" war as distant from Canada. Conflicts in Europe and Asia were thousands of miles away from North America. But Vancouver had blackouts, and most of the extensive English Bay beaches were out of bounds to civilians. Gun emplacements replaced bathers for the duration.

We should also remember that the war years showed an unexpected side of Canadian attitudes. In Coulthard's neighbourhood, there would have been several Japanese-Canadian families. Indeed, she might have met in the street the parents of Joy Kogawa, the remarkable Canadian novelist who would later tell the horrid story of the internment of Japanese-Canadian families in 1942. In that

The cottage on Wiltshire Street

year, the Canadian government used the War Measures Act to justify the removal of all persons of Japanese ancestry from any region within 100 miles of the Pacific Coast.

How did a developing composer respond to the war? Like such composers as Vaughan Williams and Copland, Coulthard wrote topical works with implied propaganda value. For example, the concert overture *Convoy* was written for Benjamin's Promenade Concerts. Today the music is reminiscent of a 1940s movie score, complete with descriptive evocations of cold winds and heroic actions. (Coulthard felt a personal connection to her theme. As the war progressed, her husband joined the Navy, and his brother Kenneth was to command a sub-hunting destroyer in North Atlantic convoys.) *Convoy* was quickly taken up by the Toronto Symphony Orchestra under Sir Ernest MacMillan, and recorded on a 78-RPM album. In peace-time, Coulthard temporarily renamed the work "Song to the Sea," hoping to extend the work's popularity beyond its role as a wartime *pièce d'occasion*. Later in life, she preferred the original title, recognizing the piece was a snapshot of a singular moment and a relatively unsophisticated demonstration of her prowess as an orchestral composer.

Coulthard eventually acquired a deeper understanding of what it meant to create art in "our war century." If it felt right to contribute a heroic orchestral piece during the war years, it felt even more right decades later to compose a threnody quartet for the souls lost in the conflict. That definitive statement took years of thought and reflection.

Although travel (like many other things in wartime) was rationed, Coulthard in 1942 resumed her study trips. She was making the most of her limited opportunities, seeking contact with some of the greatest figures in twentieth-century music. In keeping with her life-long devotion to French music, she sought out Darius Milhaud, who was working during the War at Mills College, an attractive, privately-endowed university for women in suburban San Francisco. The opportunity to meet with a member of the famous French Six composers proved irresistible. Coulthard was impressed by Milhaud's "polytonal" approach to harmony (bonding together two or more keys or chord forms to create fresh, new sonorities), and by his remarkable productivity. Here was an artist getting down to work each and every day, producing music however well or badly he might feel in body or in mind.

Coulthard continued south to Los Angeles, where she approached Arnold Schoenberg for lessons. Although Schoenberg was one of the foremost twentieth-century composers, he was a controversial, even neglected figure in the 1940s. German-occupied Europe banned performance and publication of his music. In America he was generally considered too radical, experimental, and difficult for performers and audiences. Coulthard was warmly received by the "inventor" of 12-tone music. He generously offered to send several Coulthard compositions to his publisher, George Schirmer and Company of New York.

G. SCHIRMER'S EDITION OF
STUDY SCORES
ARNOLD
SCHOENBERG
FOURTH
STRING
QUARTET
Op. 37
To Mrs Jean Coulthard Adams
cordially
Arnold Schoenberg
August 1942
G. SCHIRMER, Inc.
NEW YORK

A gift from Arnold Schoenberg

At one of their last sessions, Coulthard finally confided that she had tried using Schoenberg's 12-tone system but had not been pleased with the results. Schoenberg was not at all surprised, commenting that a student would need years of directed study of traditional repertoire before advancing productively to serial technique. He warmly encouraged Coulthard to develop her own idiom. For her part, Coulthard thought that

> [m]any composers have claimed that the serial system freed them, but I myself felt just the opposite, more hampered by it. Though I have often used 12-tone themes, I have rarely felt comfortable working with strict serial ideas. But I do feel certainly one of the best results of the serial period was the telescoping of form, pruning music back to a smaller scale from the enormously extended forms of the late 19th-century music. (MWL)

By the summer of 1942, Coulthard's domestic life changed irreversibly. Don had joined the Royal Canadian Navy that year, and been posted to Prince Rupert far up the British Columbia coast just at the Alaskan border. Only weeks after Don's departure, Jean found she was pregnant. Unfortunately, the momentous news coincided with the early days of Canadian government mail censorship. The censors were particularly suspicious of correspondence to and from naval officers, and still more suspicious about letters referring to children and to pregnancy. A coyly worded phone call about the weather got the message across.

Don and Jean's only child, daughter Jane, was born 24 May 1943 in Vancouver General Hospital. After the customary period of

Jean Coulthard with Jane, 1943

"lying-in," Jean took her newborn back to the cottage on Wiltshire Street. Doris, a day-nurse who looked the part in her starched whites, had been engaged to help Jean, who was coping, as so many women at home in war-time, on her own.

Coulthard was determined to attend to her career, daughter or not. However encouraging her study trips had been, short-term contacts could not provide the knowledge and technique Coulthard knew she required. She had moved far from the traditions of the Royal College, and was advancing past the ideas and practices of Arthur Benjamin into her own territory. She knew she had missed basic compositional ground-work along the way.

Coulthard decided to move to New York — like London, a great musical centre. By 1944, her private teaching had almost ceased. Apart from her continuing connection with Babs — preoccupied with her own four children in then-distant West Vancouver — Jean felt free to think about leaving Vancouver. Don had been posted to the Canadian Maritimes by this time, a day's train journey from New York City, and there was in any case a family connection. Coulthard would spend the winter in New York with an aunt and grandmother living near Columbia University in a little apartment. As she noted, this move "proved to be a turning point in my musical life." (MWL) She worked with Bernard Wagenaar, one of the principal composition teachers at the Juilliard School, and at that time one of the few figures who encouraged women composers. Wagenaar himself had been encouraged by the American composer Amy Cheney Beach, and had taught an eager Canadian student-composer from Winnipeg, Barbara Pentland.

Coulthard revered her new teacher:

> Wagenaar was a wonderful man, very good with his students and very attached to them, and we worked very hard for him. Later on, at UBC, I based my teaching on Wagenaar's way of doing it. (JC/WB 24 April 1995)

Wagenaar put Coulthard through a crash course in the craft of musical composition, building up her sense of form from the simple four-bar phrase on through the great traditional forms of theme-

Bernard Wagenaar

and-variation, rondo, sonata-allegro, simultaneously stretching her sense of harmony to include polytonality and twelve-tone writing.

He could not have had a more appreciative and hardworking student. Jean realized that this was just what she needed and made quick and decisive progress, learning the building blocks of compositional technique and developing a mastery of what she always called "form," the design and structure of the established musical genres. Wagenaar gave Coulthard not just the confidence but also the technique to progress beyond short works.

> The two really outstanding teachers I've worked with, who I feel could really impart, were Bernard Wagenaar, the head of the Composition Department at the Juilliard School in New York during the

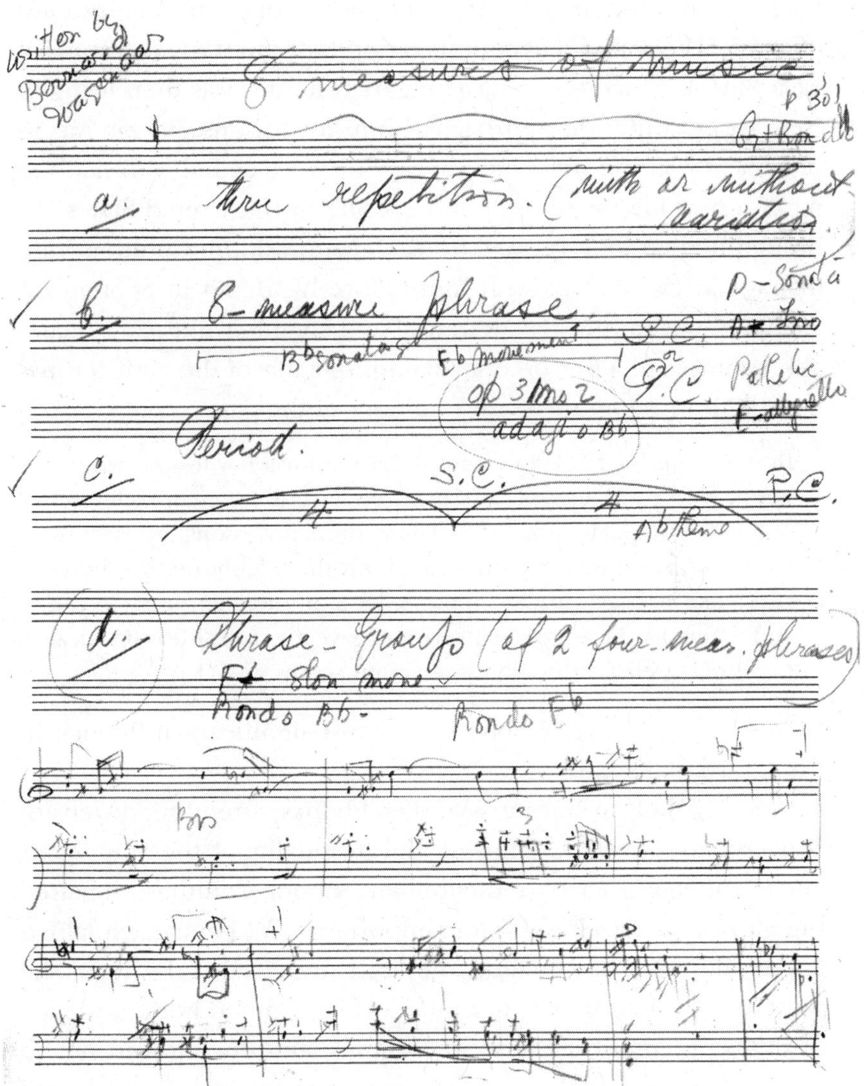

A page from Coulthard's New York workbook

1940s, and Arthur Benjamin, who lived in Canada during the war. Bernard Wagenaar had a marvellous musical mind and was a born teacher. Benjamin, on the other hand, was a delightful personality and was a tremendous help with orchestration. Also, he was in a position to perform one's works with his orchestra, conducting them himself. (MWL)

Wagenaar considered the string quartet one of the most important of classical genres and encouraged Coulthard to study the works of Béla Bartók. Since the great Hungarian master was then living in New York, Coulthard approached him for lessons. Bartók was in poor health at the time and was finding it exceedingly difficult to make a new life for himself and his wife in the United States. Although he had long refused to teach composition, Coulthard did manage a few sessions with him before his death in September, 1945 and was to find his orchestral and chamber music a remarkable example of a personal style, unmistakably of the 20th century but still drawing on the great traditions of the past.

> In the winter of 1944–45 I went to Bartók for a few lessons while I was in New York. He was *most* surprised to find a woman composer on his doorstep. He thought I'd come for piano lessons! Apparently I had not made myself clear enough on the telephone. He didn't really like to teach any composers, let alone female ones. In the end, I must say he was very sincere and gave me many ideas on aural training as well as criticizing some of my scores. (MWL)

Bartók became, after Debussy, the most significant influence in Coulthard's later work.

Working daily at her musical sketchbooks, attending dozens of concerts in New York, enjoying the hospitality of the Wagenaars and of young musicians in the Juilliard School, Coulthard repaired the gaps in her training. Most importantly, Wagenaar explained large-scale form and made Coulthard understand the logic she must develop to organize her music. He expanded her knowledge of then-contemporary harmonic idioms, and encouraged her to write for instrumental and vocal combinations which Jean had not yet tried. He showed her the day-to-day life and the work habits of a committed composer-teacher.

Coulthard had seen her childhood and adolescence as "mostly wonderful, with just a spot of difficulty now and then." As an adult living in a two-bedroom apartment with two elderly women at the end of a world war, she thought the balance of things was still about the same, "mostly wonderful." Musically speaking, it was among the best of times. The groundwork was laid for decades of productivity and sustained work. Meanwhile, in personal terms, it was a hugely demanding life: to be a mother to the little Janey, to maintain a wholehearted commitment to art, to continue a marriage (mostly by mail) in wartime — this was a test of adulthood, and perhaps no less a test than that of women in many parts of the western world in wartime.

By summer 1945, as the European theatre of war finally closed, Coulthard had acquired a solid technical foundation in the craft of musical composition, and a firm footing in the great enterprise of life.

Jean Coulthard in the 1940s

3

A NEW PROFESSIONAL LIFE

At war's end in 1945, Jean Coulthard and husband Don were anxious to return to Vancouver and, for the first time in years, a family life approaching normality. In today's terms, her musical work with Bernard Wagenaar paralleled the curriculum of a Master's program complete with thesis requirements. She now knew how to go about working her ideas into large-scale compositions. She felt a new sense of connection with the great world of twentieth-century music, and a new confidence that would sustain her long career.

Within a month of her return to Vancouver, still living in boxes and suitcases, she was composing again. As she recalled, beginning in the autumn of 1945,

> I wrote several works, some major chamber music duos and a piano sonata, in which I felt that really for the first time I had complete

Don and Janey

> control of my technique of writing. I also felt my own personal style had blossomed and my years of apprenticeship were finished — though, of course, not my years of learning, because one learns forever. (MWL)

The Vancouver to which she returned had changed artistically and culturally: Arthur Benjamin was no longer on the scene. In 1946, fed up with Vancouver, he had returned to Britain. Composers Robert Barclay and Robert Fleming had gone on to the United States and Ottawa. That left a handful of occasional church composers and writers of pop music in town. No other Vancouver musicians showed sustained commitment to the writing and performing of serious new music.

Nevertheless, new artistic ideas from Central Europe were in the air, brought by refugees to the Coast. Among them was Dr. Ida Halpern, a Viennese musicologist who studied the music of the native peoples of the Pacific Northwest and introduced the cultural study of music in her courses at UBC in the early 1940s. The Europeans were a little impatient with the provincialism of Anglo-Saxon Vancouver and its comfortable ways. Slowly, very slowly, Vancouver audiences took up new attitudes.

A prime example of change and renovation was the Vancouver Symphony, in the middle of a vital reorganization after several difficult Depression and war years. Conductor Allard de Ridder had for too long been the *only* conductor, and far too few people were making decisions on symphony programming, educational outreach, and fundraising. To many, the Symphony was a clique of narrow and self-centred socialites (not least Mrs. B.T. Rogers herself). De Ridder left in 1941, to be followed by a succession of guest conductors, among them John Barbirolli, Leonard Bernstein, Otto Klemperer, and Jean-Marie Beaudet. Given Barbirolli's and Klemperer's fame, and the rising excitement surrounding Bernstein and Beaudet, it was no surprise that VSO attendance shot up. In the 1945–1946 season alone, Vancouver heard works by Stravinsky, Schoenberg, and Hindemith.

In late summer 1946 a new phase of Coulthard's life began. Harry Adaskin, the charismatic second violin of Toronto's Hart House String Quartet (then Canada's only professional string quartet), had been hired to form a new music department at the University of British Columbia. For UBC it was a new departure, as music had been until then only an occasional feature of life at Point Grey. It had, of course, been important in the ordinary lives of students who for one reason or another presented musical dramas or other events from the University's opening in 1915 onward. Now, in 1946, Adaskin invited Coulthard to join the University's faculty and to

The charismatic Harry Adaskin

help UBC begin a new chapter in its artistic history.[10] Coulthard reminisced:

> I joined the Music Department at the University of British Columbia in 1947 and designed the first music theory course there. Little did I think I would teach there for 25 years! Frances and Harry Adaskin and myself were all young and full of enthusiasm, so I enjoyed working in the academic climate. (MWL)

At UBC Harry Adaskin worked with a tiny budget, the limited tastes of Vancouver audiences, and the primitive state of music education in the province. He decided he would not even *try* to create a true university department of music, nor to follow the American example of a university-based conservatory. Instead, building on his personal charisma, he launched a drive to popularize music in the growing student body of war veterans and musical amateurs. Adaskin's minuscule Department offered only a music appreciation course for non-musicians, and two theory courses for B.A. students taking a minor concentration in music.

Adaskin displayed only grudging commitment to the training of practical, performing musicians yet used his own cachet as a performer to advance his Department's (and his own) prestige. He would soon expand UBC's theory offerings by recruiting another composer — Barbara Pentland from Toronto — for the Department in 1949. Coulthard thought that Harry showed scant understanding of the academic side of music education.

> The funny thing is, Harry knew absolutely *nothing* about the theory of music. But I had a reputation as a composer, and a theorist. (JC/WB, 25 May 1996)

Adaskin succeeded in giving music a toehold at UBC. Over the years, generations of Vancouverites remembered his anecdote-filled Music Appreciation lectures with affection. However, during his headship, UBC was moving ahead academically. Adaskin's leisurely game plan could not possibly succeed in the new UBC. In 1958, just over a decade after his arrival, Adaskin was forced out of administration, although kept on as a Music Appreciation lecturer.[11]

Physically speaking, UBC in the late 1940s was nothing like an established eastern university. Years afterward, when she received an honorary doctorate from UBC, Coulthard mentioned the acres of mud and construction that greeted her in 1925 and again in 1947, and still . . . in 1988. Between 1915 and the outbreak in 1939 of war, UBC student numbers hovered at 1,500. After 1946 they quadrupled, to just under 6,000.

For more than a decade teaching and almost all faculty and student accommodation was in abandoned army huts on the windswept Point Grey peninsula, miles from Vancouver's downtown. No thought had been given to the physical needs of the Department of Music, but everyone muddled on. Coulthard even gave lessons and tutorials in her little Austin, patriotically chosen to help support the recovery of British industry.

It is hard to see how Coulthard could have fit in with Adaskin's original scheme for music at the University. At this juncture, she valued professional training too much to accept Adaskin's well-meaning but vague ideas of an attractive curriculum for amateurs. She also saw that she would have to make changes in her own orientation, knowing she could not single-handedly change UBC. In 1949 she stopped her occasional local piano performances, settled down to teaching elementary harmony to huge undergraduate classes, and made a life as an artist *outside* the university. Her compositions appeared on an occasional Wednesday noon UBC recital program, or in one of the violin-piano evenings that Harry Adaskin and his wife, Frances Marr, organized on campus. She was not unlike any number of composers across Europe and North America whose bread and butter came from college, university, or conser-

Post-War UBC huts

vatory teaching, but whose spiritual and artistic sustenance came from a wider world of art and artists.[12]

Coulthard was on the move, but on a trajectory of her own. She paid little or no attention to the example of her new composer colleague in the Department — even though Barbara Pentland's "office" was a desk across the room. After years of working on her own, Coulthard might have welcomed a true composer-colleague, but by style and temperament, Coulthard and Pentland were destined to misunderstanding. Pentland's quest for originality drew her to an increasingly radical idiom, and an aggressively confrontational stance that challenged conventional taste. Coulthard knew her Vancouver audience and wished to charm them into understanding her brand of modernism. There was to be no common ground for the next five decades. She and Pentland would agree to disagree.

Unlike many of her university colleagues of the 1960s, Coulthard did not press for advancement. She was hired in the relatively modest rank of Lecturer and advanced only as far as Senior Lecturer with a form of tenure. In retirement, after twenty-six years' service, faced with a shockingly modest pension, she realized the full cost of her earlier decision. But a choice between university politics and composition could only have gone one way.

While adding teaching duties at UBC to her life, Coulthard continued the sustained artistic activity she had begun in New York under Bernard Wagenaar's supervision. Her 1945 four piano *Etudes* had a Vancouver public performance in 1948. That year saw completion of her first major work for choir, *Quebec May*. The lyrical *Music on a Quiet Song* for flute and string orchestra (1946) displayed a willingness to apply lessons learned from Benjamin and Wagenaar: from the one, writing for orchestra (whether or not an orchestra would ever play the music), from the other, the use of large-scale forms.

THE MUSIC: *Quebec May* (1948)

Quebec May, composed in January 1948, remains one of Coulthard's most popular choral works. In several later talks Coulthard said that at the end of the Second World War there was a feeling of "springtime" in the arts in Canada. *Quebec May* is filled with a sense of new beginnings and shows the still-developing composer finding her voice.

The work is designed for good amateur or school choirs and two pianos.

Coulthard thought that with large choirs, a single piano accompaniment was often lost and ineffective. Two pianos were better able to match a robust choral sound. In *Quebec May* the keyboard writing is flamboyant and rhythmically exciting, and requires pianists who shine as soloists, not accompanists.

For her text Coulthard turned to the work of her University of British Columbia colleague Earle Birney. Like the composer, Birney was an artist beginning his long career, just starting to attract national attention as a poet. Birney's poem sketches an impression of the Quebec countryside in spring.

Later in her career Coulthard might have chosen a more elaborate form for a major work like this, but here the structure is simple in several broad sections. The music begins tentatively with polychords melting together in the two pianos.

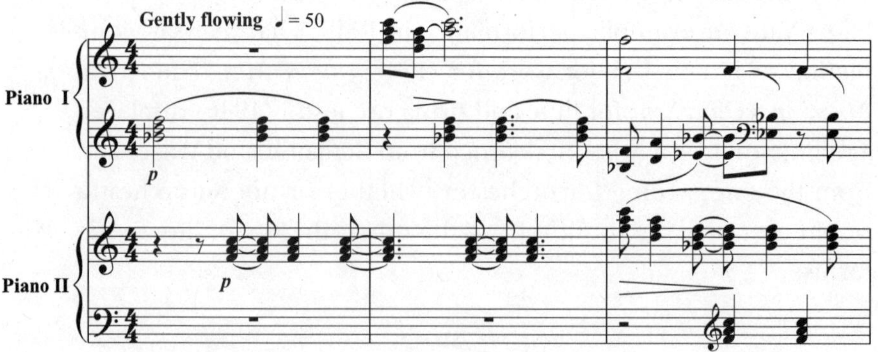

The choir enters with the words "Now the snow is vanished clean."

A gentle fugato theme reflects the text "Skyward point the cedar billows, / Birches pinken, poplars green":

This theme was a Coulthard favourite; she used it again in her 1974 orchestral work *Canada Mosaic.* Further short sections alternate lyrical and more scherzo-like materials.

In the middle of the work the tempo accelerates. Even the old farm horse feels the magic of spring: "Even Telesphore is frisky, vieux Telesphore, holà!" A last quiet glimpse backward at the opening chords leads to the end section — a toccata for the two pianos underlying the words "racing on the springing land" and a brilliant, rhythmic close.

Quebec May was an immediate success, winning an important prize from the CBC, performances, and even a recording with a young Mario Bernardi (who was later to conduct so many Coulthard works with the CBC Radio Orchestra) playing one of the piano parts.

Although Coulthard would write many further choral works, from short part-songs and works for junior choir to her massive *Choral Symphony: This Land. Quebec May* was always a favourite work with choirs, conductors, pianists, and audience. In 1987 Elmer Eisler asked Coulthard to work on a version for choir and orchestra, and after forty years she returned to the work, orchestrating the first sections herself and asking former pupil Frederick Schipizky to try his hand at the final section. The new version of the work was recorded (1988) by the CBC.

In the post-war years 1946–1947 Coulthard produced three important sonatas for solo piano, oboe and piano, and cello and piano. Although she did not realize it at the time, these works were to be the cornerstone of a long series of sonatas for almost all instruments. The 1946–1947 sonatas combine traditional formal design with what Coulthard habitually called polytonal harmony. After her lessons with Wagenaar, she adopted sonata-form first movements, binary or ternary slow movements, and rondo-like finales — a sequence of movements that appeared and reappeared in her work from then on. Her "polytonality" in fact was a bonding of major and minor triad forms; this bonding created new harmonies that worked well in characteristic Coulthard-style figurations — an effective blend of the advanced and the familiar.[13] Listeners without a background in theory might not have understood what Coulthard was up to, but responded instinctively to the freshness of her idiom. She wrote for herself as much as for the Vancouver musicians she knew. She embraced her new responsibilities as a university teacher, but she wasn't about to let slide her commitment to composing.

> During this time of my life I usually worked at night, which I found peaceful and seemed to agree with me perfectly. I would usually begin about 9 p.m. and continue into the small hours of the morning. (CWS)

With *his* post-war return to civilian life, Coulthard's husband found that his plans for a new career in design and decoration were also taking shape. Don Adams began his career as an interior

The music room on Wiltshire

designer and importer of furniture in the late 1940s. With two increasingly regular incomes, the family's domestic arrangements stabilized.

In order to have time for creative projects, she needed and wanted help. In the old days, before the Depression and the war, all Vancouver families in the Coulthards' circle had servants, often several. By the 1950s, it was much more unusual. Coulthard spent a significant portion of her UBC salary on domestic help, thus making time for composition. She began a regime of disciplined work that would last the rest of her life, embarking on projects that expanded her powers as a composer.

> In the 1950s I began to feel that my earlier lyrical style was not enough to encompass the depth of my thought, and I began to write works which stretched further harmonically and deeper emotionally. (MWL)

These "deeper" works included the *First Symphony* (1950), the *Duo Sonata* (1952) for violin and piano, and the *Variations on BACH* (1952) for piano solo. Writing a first string quartet (1952) was a landmark for Coulthard. The history of music is filled with examples of composers' trepidation about string quartets and symphonies. Coulthard shared these anxieties.

> When I was in my mid-thirties, Bernard Wagenaar, the great teacher of music composition at the Juilliard School in those years, once asked me how I felt about writing a string quartet. I replied that I had neither the courage or fortitude. We then agreed it is really the highest form of musical expression — the essence of music expressed by divine strings. The tradition and forms set by the past great masters leave one with a sense of awe and wonder. . . .

Like many musicians, Coulthard saw the string quartet as the defining genre of chamber music. Now in her forties, she began to think she might be ready to write her first. Chamber music was gaining prominence in Canada. Coulthard was delighted when Toronto's Solway Quartet offered her a $50 commission to write for them. "I thought it was the beautiful sound of these strings that had put my 'Divine Discontent' to the challenge."

She would write two further string quartets, as well as her chamber music masterwork, *Octet: Twelve Essays on a Cantabile Theme.* The first quartet is the more traditional.

> My *First Quartet* is, I think, very lyrical in sound. Presently, I feel I have in a rather vague way two styles of writing — a lyrical vein which, however, always remains in my more serious or profound style of writing. It was a Quartet "In the Spring of the year," and owes some to Debussy (perhaps everybody's first Quartet does) even the great Bartók. (DD)

The quartet is unusual since it can be either three or four movements long. Coulthard dithered about the scherzo after receiving criticism implying that her original was derivative; she wrote a second one, then decided either (or neither) could be performed.

If writing a string quartet was fairly ambitious, writing a full-length symphony in the early 1950s was just plain rash. There were few Canadian orchestras, and even fewer prepared to program such a work. More practical composers turned to small orchestral pieces or film music. But Coulthard was committed to the idea of the great forms of classical music and knew it was time to try to create a symphony of her own.

In writing her *First Symphony,* Coulthard adopted style elements from Paul Hindemith, then at the height of his influence in North America. She rejected both the expressionism of Schoenberg and Stravinsky's brand of late neo-classicism, opting for Hindemith-inspired sober orchestration, expanded yet tonal harmony, and emphasis on counterpoint. The Symphony was well enough received, given a prize by the Australian Broadcasting Commission and publicly performed by the Toronto Symphony Orchestra under Ettore Mazzolini. But Coulthard's flirtation with Hindemith did not last long. She had to find her own way.

As Coulthard was embracing (then rejecting) Hindemith, other Canadians were finally discovering modernism. Post-war Vancouver artists led the rest of the country in their willingness to espouse modernist values. Coulthard's friend and UBC colleague B.C. Binning had designed and built one of the first truly modern homes in the country in a forest clearing in West Vancouver. Painter Jack Shadbolt rapidly moved from realism to expressionism, surrealism and abstraction. Canada's greatest architect, Arthur Erickson, was designing his first projects. Despite shortages of housing, the baby boom, and other post-war problems, the Vancouver spirit was optimistic.

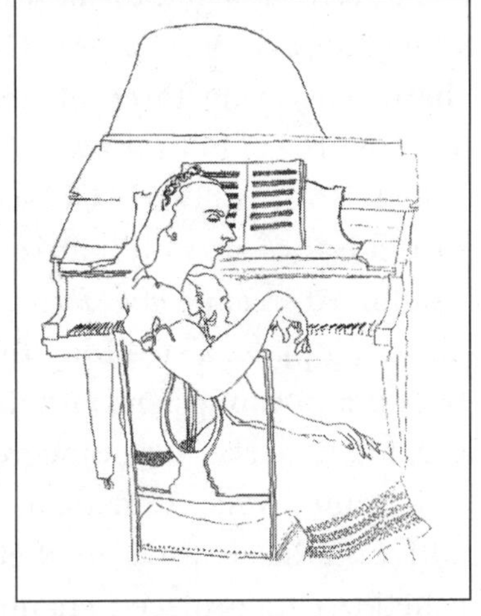

Jean Coulthard by B.C. Binning

Even Vancouver's conservative musical circles showed willingness to consider new forms of expression. In 1950 Vancouver hosted the First Symposium of Canadian Contemporary Music, "the largest festival of Canadian music" to that date. During the 1950s, Canadian musicians found new opportunities through broadcasting. Radio, then television flourished through the French and English networks of the CBC and Radio-Canada International.

That same decade saw the establishment of organizations specifically designed to help Canadian music. Since the war, as Coulthard's letters show, she had seen the advantages of a national composers' group. She was delighted to be asked by Toronto composer-teacher John Weinzweig to be a founding member of the Canadian League of Composers.

> One of the great aims of the Canadian League of Composers is to promote performances of music written by Canadians. I find it very stimulating that composers are now ready and willing to work together, and become their *own* concert managers, in other words, to do something about presenting performances *themselves* of their own music rather than merely continuing to deplore the state of affairs! (THYC)

Publishers began to show increased interest in serious work by Canadian composers: BMI Canada was the first to publish Coulthard, engraving three of her *Etudes* in 1952, and the fourth in 1954. Three of her *Preludes* for piano came out in 1959, the last two called "Torment" and "Quest," another sign of emotional and musical advance in Coulthard's accelerating career. BMI published Coulthard's *Four Piano Pieces,* dedicated "to [daughter] Jane and all young players," realizing that Coulthard's work might appeal to baby-boom youngsters, and thus lead to modest profits in the tiny Canadian market for homegrown classical music.

In time, other Canadian and international publishers would add Coulthard works to their catalogues: Waterloo Music published teaching pieces, chamber works, and a number of orchestral compositions; Frederick Harris, associated with the Royal Conservatory, became another major exponent of her educational music, while the respected British publisher Novello took keyboard and chamber works. Oxford University Press distributed junior choral works, again in line with the firm's long tradition in that field. By the 1990s regional publishers — Alberta Keys in Calgary and Avondale Music in North Vancouver among others —

produced editions for specific audiences and included Coulthard in their catalogues.

Another crucial musical foundation of the late 1950s was the Canadian Music Centre, a national circulating library of scores by Canada's "serious" composers. It opened first in Toronto, and then established branches in all Canadian regions. Where commercial and educational publishing left off, the Canadian Music Centre took over, giving Canadians a means of seeing and using the works of their own composers, especially those works that existed only in manuscript form.

Four Piano Pieces

With hindsight it is possible to find touchstones in Jean Coulthard's professional life. In the late 1920s Coulthard worked with a renowned composer in a great musical city. The key to the 1930s was the traumatic death of her mother, the end of an idyllic, extended adolescence. In the 1940s, she solidified her craft and accepted a remunerative appointment in a university. She extended her compositional range from small piano pieces to sonatas, from songs to quartets and symphonies.

Jean Coulthard by Françoise André

Maturity came to Jean Coulthard in the mid-1940s. By the 1950s, she thought of herself as a hard-working composer, beginning to have recognition and acclaim.

Jean Coulthard in the 1950s

4

A YEAR IN FRANCE

By coincidence, Jean Coulthard made the acquaintance of one of her most significant professional and personal friends toward the end of the 1940s through her friends Lawren and Bess Harris. One of the original Group of Seven Canadian painters, Harris had lived in Vancouver since 1940 with his second wife Bess.

The Harris home, perched above the beach at Spanish Banks near the University, became an informal meeting-point for people interested in the arts and in new ideas. Bess Harris was the dedicatee of the first of Coulthard's *Preludes* for piano. Coulthard recalled how

> [i]n those days Lawren Harris had come west with his new wife Bess Harris. There was a terrible Toronto scandal over that, but Bess & I and Lawren were all wonderful friends. They used to put on magnificent dinners and parties at their house. (JC/WB 22 January 1994)

Elizabeth Poston

At a Harris dinner party in May 1948, there was a surprise guest: Miss Elizabeth Poston from Hertfordshire, England.[14] Poston was in British Columbia for a "rest cure" with friends on Saltspring Island — quite a change from her normal life, in an English house made famous by E.M. Forster's novel *Howards End.*

Coulthard quickly learned why Poston needed that rest. Poston had run a BBC radio service from London throughout most of World War II, broadcasting coded musical instructions and warnings. Margaret Ashby writes that

> [t]he harsh realities of war were thrust in front of Elizabeth when she was recalled to London, to undertake new duties for the BBC at Bush House. Here she did secret service work, carrying out an idea thought to have been originated by Churchill, whereby gramo-

"Howards End"

> phone records were used to broadcast coded messages to resistance movements in Europe. Although she received instructions from a superior, she was the only person actually to operate the system. It was a nerve-wracking business; if she had played a wrong tune, she could have caused the people of some Nazi-occupied country to rise against their oppressors too soon, to meet certain destruction. To the end of her life she had recurrent nightmares in which this happened.[15]

All this was "wildly exciting" to Coulthard. She knew something of military matters, as her husband Don had spent most of the war in the Navy, and his brother Kenneth was a naval Lieutenant-Commander. Sitting at dinner next to a woman who had engaged indirectly in espionage was stimulating indeed.

Still better, Poston was an established English composer and scholar known for her work on seventeenth- and eighteenth-century musical manuscripts. She was well-connected in London's vocal and instrumental musical life, and linked informally with the

A Poston Edition

esteemed song-composer and critic Peter Warlock (pseudonym for Philip Heseltine). She was about to help create the famous Third Programme for the BBC. Later Poston would edit a best-selling carol collection, write one of the most popular twentieth-century carols ("Jesus Christ the Apple Tree"), and become a pioneer of the British Women Composers' Society.[16]

Coulthard and Poston became immediate close friends, and remained in contact for over three decades. Nearly all of Poston's letters and cards to Coulthard over a thirty-five-year friendship have survived (although Coulthard's side of the correspondence has not). Knowing she would have a good British welcome, she made the first of fifteen trans-Atlantic treks, often to see Poston, even more often to hear her music "done" at festivals and recitals in the United Kingdom and on the Continent. As these journeys became faster and cheaper, Coulthard made the most of her opportunities.

She rarely complained about the effects of frequent journeys across the Atlantic — fatigue or a temporary shortage of cash at home.

Coulthard travelled for friendship, but even more to participate in the revitalizing whirl of British and Continental musical life. Summer 1949 was Coulthard's first visit to "Howards End" (Rook's Nest House, Stevenage, Hertfordshire). Over the next five years, the records show Coulthard in England, Scotland, and France. In 1952, the year Elizabeth II became Queen, Coulthard enjoyed a summer journey with Poston through southern England and in the south of France, partly for music, mostly for fun. Poston was conveniently francophone and thoroughly familiar with European roads. Poston's way of introducing Coulthard to *her* Europe had a certain romantic drama. She insisted that Jean's first glimpse of Venice should be in the old manner, by boat, late at night. Jean and Elizabeth sailed through the shadowy canals of *la Serenissima.* Jean was, of course, charmed.

On a subsequent trip, Jean felt she had to see Vita Sackville-West's garden at Sissinghurst. It was before the days of National Trust ownership. Sackville-West and her author-diplomat husband, Harold Nicolson, were in residence. Jean had to be content with a glimpse over the hedge. But at that moment, Coulthard and Poston were discovered by none other than Vita herself. Coulthard, as a colonial, was welcomed and shown around. For Poston, who travelled in Sackville-West's artistic circles, to be found like a common tourist was something of an embarrassment.

By 1953 short summer trips were not enough. Coulthard found long years of teaching, composition, endless business (especially finding publishers and performers), family responsibility, and domestic life were taking a toll. These factors — teaching, creative work, and family — played a part in Coulthard's decision to try to take an entire year abroad, away from Canada, away from UBC, away from home.

To see why Coulthard welcomed the possibility of a full year away (her first since the New York winter of 1944–1945), it helps to recall — once again — how Canadian music developed in the 1940s and

1950s. Modernism, late to take root, became the musical style. The older generation, represented by a Sir Ernest MacMillan, a Healey Willan, or a Claude Champagne, were still prominent and politically influential in Canada's small musical community. But a new generation of Canadian composers, by then early-middle-aged, were moving in new directions.

Through Depression and war, Canadian composers had been geographically scattered, functioning in solitude. Some came to think they had made important creative breakthroughs in their lives and work, yet there was little sense of community or solidarity among them.

> I now realize the '40s were a crucial decade in the development of music in the East of Canada. But frankly, during the early '40s we were rather unaware of the progress of new ideas in Toronto and Montreal. Our outlook in Vancouver was either to Europe or the U.S., and we only later became aware of the struggle going on in the East. (JCCM)

Vancouverites came into direct contact with recent developments in Canadian serious music when the city hosted the First Symposium of Canadian Contemporary Music in 1950. Thirty composers were featured, Coulthard among them, although few representatives from Quebec bothered to come all the way to Vancouver, and the males of the newly minted "Toronto School" dominated the gathering. Factional differences between Toronto, Montreal, and western attitudes to composition were revealed. Harry Somers, Harry Freedman, and their teacher John Weinzweig were fusing neoclassical and serial techniques, creating a recognizable "northern" brand of mid-century modernism. Coulthard's impressionist-derived idiom was not in step.

After 1945, forward-looking composers had begun to explore electronic music and took renewed interest in serialism, especially that of Schoenberg's one-time pupil Anton Webern. Composers whose work did not adapt were dismissed as old fashioned and irrelevant. In England, Benjamin Britten's work was under fire; in the United States Aaron Copland, at the height of his fame, reluctantly adopted serial procedures but then composed less and less. When Igor Stravinsky embraced serial technique (after the death of his life-long rival, Schoenberg), composers everywhere had to take stock. Less than ten years before, Coulthard had discussed serialism in her lessons with Schoenberg. He encouraged her to continue in her own way. She was convinced the new fads and techniques were not for her; she would keep to the aesthetic values of the earlier French modernists and of Bartók.

In the 1950 Symposium, and in the particular and narrow modernism of the 1950s, there was reason for celebration and for regret. There was reason to celebrate the growing energy of Canadian "serious" music, but also reason to worry about the fads and fetishes that threatened to envelop it.

Coulthard's disquiet intensified for a purely professional reason: new difficulties with her employer and boss. Wanting always to be up-to-date, Harry Adaskin had taken to adding "surprise" courses to the curriculum, new public programming for transient musicians, and various internal "administrative reforms." Then the unthinkable happened:

> Harry Adaskin called over to see us one night and said he "wouldn't require my services any more." In other words, he'd like to fire me. We were so shocked. . . . I was horrified he would do such a thing. Nobody could account for Harry's action. I was a great friend of [Dean] Geoff Andrews and of President MacKenzie and knew them well. So I fought it! (JC/WB 8 January 1994)

Coulthard felt betrayed. It looked as though Adaskin wished to jettison his "traditionalist" to entrench further the position of his "radical" protégée, Barbara Pentland.

Questions of fairness apart, Coulthard's family *needed* the regular income her UBC job provided, especially as she had gradually given up her private piano and theory teaching and had committed herself to UBC. By 1949, the last of her private piano pupils was gone. The little garage studio on Wiltshire was quiet. Beyond her few performance fees each year, Coulthard had no reliable way to bring in funds.

Don Adams

Coulthard kept her job, but life in the UBC Department of Music became a trial. She had lost confidence in Harry Adaskin's vision, and was exasperated by her inability to effect productive administrative or curricular change. Although she kept on producing new compositions, she was in the middle of a creative crisis and in acute need of guidance and support. She needed space, time, and detachment to consider her career objectives.

She remembered her mother's many trips for professional renewal. She also saw the example of her own husband, then in the building stages of his own post-war career. His "Don Adams Interiors" would prosper in the later 1950s and 1960s. With an astute eye, Adams anticipated the public interest in Danish furniture in the mid-1950s, and the fascination with things Spanish in the

Don Adams Interiors

1960s. He was an appreciative and receptive student of Asian art and furnishings, using Japanese and Chinese ideas of space to help him think about the design of his own houses and gardens, and the houses and gardens of his clients. Extensive business travel was a part of his life. Adams's letters show him travelling around the world on business in the 1950s, 1960s, and early 1970s.

In the middle decades of the twentieth century, travel was becoming ever easier, but still took time, money, and effort. Costs were relatively high in the postwar inflation of the early 1950s, although beginning to come down by 1954. A ticket to England in 1952 or 1953 easily cost two to three months of the earnings of a UBC lecturer. Even when the time factor changed completely with the introduction of jetliners in the late 1950s, the other considerations remained.

Coulthard now applied for and won a Royal Society of Canada Fellowship (precursor to the Canada Council grants of the 1960s

Coulthard's Paris address in the rue d'Assas

and later). It would finance a year in France — an interlude in Coulthard's life that she later called a "princely gift." She started in summer 1955 with a brief stay in England. Her twelve-year-old daughter, Janey, arrived in time for school term, September 1955, in Paris.

> For the first six months my daughter and I settled in Paris in a pension on the rue d'Assas. One could write a saga on the ups and downs of pension life. But I have one treasured vision of the petite elderly Madame who owned the pension with her rather crusty and pennythrift daughter. It was a typical French scene as gentle Madame

> sat at the head of the long table, surrounded by her guests and with the tall red wine bottles standing like sentinels-at-arms as one good French dish after another was served to us. When I think of that winter in Paris so many vivid recollections flash — the vendors roasting chestnuts on the street corners with the grey smoke twirling skyward — the walks in the Luxembourg gardens to watch the charming French children at their games or to gaze at and admire the tall statues of the Queens of France. We had weekend excursions by train out of Paris for woodland walks. . . . Or perhaps we would go on pilgrimages especially sacred to me, to Saint Germain-en-Laye to see the Maillol statue of Debussy in the park of his birthplace or to Montfort L'Amaury to glimpse Ravel's last, quaint house. One could indeed imagine Ravel enjoying his hobby — mechanical toys — here! Again in Paris itself, who could ever forget the soft snow flakes falling on the Louvre an evening near Christmas. (AYIF)

France posed linguistic and logistical problems but offered a life under untroubled skies. Janey was put into school, a piano found for work, and the rudiments of language brushed up. It was no holiday for mother or daughter, as both worked to make sure Janey got through the ordeal of a foreign schooling. Janey's homework became Jean Coulthard's as well:

> In the daylight hours I could work until 4 p.m. when Jane returned from school. . . . The French schools laid it on very thick! We learned arithmetic — *calcul* — as a team. And at the end of term, Jane received the "Tableau d'honneur" for the student in the class who had "tried the hardest." *Who* won that "Tableau d'honneur"? (AYIF)

When she was not working, Coulthard explored Paris, heard new works by prominent composers of the day, and made little pilgrimages outside the city. A highlight was the premiere of Darius Milhaud's opera *Bolívar.* Coulthard's meeting with well-established composer Jean Françaix was less successful. "[He] made it perfectly clear that he wasn't the least bit interested in knowing a composer from Canada." But the most magical coincidence was hearing the great Marcel Dupré in the organ loft at St.-Sulpice, just around from the pension, in the select company of his family, students, and distinguished friend Albert Schweitzer.

The interior at St.-Sulpice

There was much to be learned in the City of Light. The Coulthard Papers for autumn 1955 include some dark blue forms covered with smudgy pencilled names and numbers. These are the borrowing slips of Jean Coulthard for private research in the Special Collections and Manuscripts department of the Bibliothèque Nationale, then in the rue Richelieu in central Paris. One is for a volume on harmony and counterpoint by Jean-Philippe Rameau, another for an original print of Palestrina's *Missarum liber secundus*

(Rome, 1567) — we have Coulthard's notes on the placement of voices in this music, and of course, its polyphony.

> To gain entrée into the ancient manuscript room was like trying to force one's way in to see the Crown Jewels. Letters were required from the Canadian Embassy, besides my passport, and endless other documents to be filled in. Finally I was ushered into a dark and quiet room, off to the side of the main Reading Room. The guardians asked me, gravely and repeatedly, what reasons I could possibly have for handling their precious books. A half-hour passed. They could not think why I would want to see the books, but they could not think of a strong reason to deny me. The guardians produced a lovely wooden box full of white gloves. Then a third group of guardians arrived bearing the Palestrina volumes. I spent the morning turning the pages — wearing white gloves — and feeling as if Giovanni Pierluigi da Palestrina's spirit was hovering in one of the darker corners, and smiling. (AYIF)

There was a whole continent of musical knowledge at the Bibliothèque Nationale, another in Parisian concert halls, and still another in the salons of the day. Since the mid-seventeenth century, the learned and the wealthy (sometimes the same people) had organized weekly or monthly gatherings of intellectuals and artists in Paris receiving rooms. For the young, it was an opportunity to meet and to learn from their artistic and intellectual elders (and also to be warm and well fed for an evening or an afternoon). For older artists, it was a question of stimulation. Coulthard knew, as most North American musicians did, that an important musical salon was still flourishing in the 1950s in the apartments of world-renowned teacher Nadia Boulanger at her flat near the Place Pigalle. Coulthard made her pilgrimage to see "Madame," as had Aaron Copland, Leonard Bernstein, and many others since the 1920s. Alas, Coulthard found Boulanger unsympathetic.

> My first impression of her was a very small, dreary, non-descript woman dressed all in black, including even her stockings. But once she spoke — the strong illumination of her personality was evident as if the lights were suddenly switched on. (AYIF)

Evenings with Madame were heavy and long, as people listened to her lengthy discourses on music, culture, and politics. The rooms were "laden with bric-a-brac souvenirs" and flowers from adoring friends.

> Nadia Boulanger sat — the centre-piece for everyone vivaciously carrying on and steering the Gallic stream of wit and conversation. (AYIF)

Boulanger was the first and last woman with whom Coulthard studied composition.

> She was *not* a composer and there is the great difference in comparison with others I have worked with. "Lili," her sister, some years gone, *was* the composer, and I recall a little picture of her fastened to one side of the music rack on the grand piano. Her adored sister always in front of her seemed to me a very touching thing. . . . The telephone would ring sometimes and it would be "my dear friend Stravinsky" or "my dear friend Malipiero!" (AYIF)

The highlight of her Paris winter was a concert of Canadian music conducted by the great Gaston Poulet, the last musician to perform with Debussy.

> The works were apparently chosen in Canada and on the first draft I was not included. Then, to my utter astonishment, Mr. René Garneau, the cultural affairs attaché at the Canadian Embassy, telephoned me and asked to see *more* Canadian scores. Fortunately, I had brought several, and to my great pleasure *Ballade "A Winter's Tale"* was scheduled.
>
> Janey clutched my hand all through the performance. The few friends we had made in Paris all attended the concert and it was a case of "my cup runneth over," for after the performance M. Poulet wrote to me: "You write beautiful music."
>
> What a happy ending, on the point of departure from Paris, an evening our friends celebrated with champagne! (AYIF)

From late January to June 1956, Jean and Jane lived on the Mediterranean coast, near Menton, at Roquebrune. The weather was far better, and in any case, Menton had been a social and artistic retreat for centuries. Coulthard may have heard about this beautiful region from Canadians, possibly from Jack Shadbolt, a UBC artist who was already trying to obtain a fellowship to stay in Menton the year after Coulthard's "sabbatical." B.C. and Jessie Binning and George and Inge Woodcock, all with UBC connections, had stayed in the region. Earle Birney had won the very same scholarship for a year (calendar year 1953) in France, and spent

Roquebrune-Village

An unhappy birthday in France as seen by Janey: in bed with the flu

much of it in Antibes, a few kilometres west of Roquebrune. Coulthard's *Quebec May* and *Vancouver Lights* used texts by Birney, and the two had been colleagues at UBC for years.

Roquebrune-Village is a ten-minute drive from the Italian border, and built on a steep mountainside above the Mediterranean. The locals affected an interest in the requirement of artists for peaceful places in which to create. Coulthard went straight to work as soon as a rented piano could be found, and people with strong enough backs to bring the instrument up the steep hill to her little house. There she began her full-length opera, *The Return of the Native,* based on the novel by Thomas Hardy. The opera was completed twenty years later.

On the last leg of a round-the-world buying trip, husband Don (no Francophile) dropped in at Roquebrune in late May. The reunited family was off to Italy for museums and concerts. It was an agreeable ending to a productive and encouraging year.

Altogether, "the year in France" was a near-apotheosis for a woman whose youth had been shaped by French music. Indeed, since the turn of the twentieth century, the Coulthard women had been only slightly less francophile than anglophile. Now Jean had lived at the source. Daughter Janey came along because her parents thought a year in Europe a good thing for anyone at any age.

The journey home to tiny, distant, rainy Vancouver must have been anticlimactic. But there were compensations. Don had decorated a fine new house on Vancouver's posh South West Marine Drive, a house that would become a testing ground for Don's design theories and enthusiasms. Besides, Coulthard's Canadian musical reputation had not suffered in her absence. Her particular brand of mid-century modernism was finding supporters, and she maintained a place in Vancouver's musical networks.

THE MUSIC: *Spring Rhapsody* (1958)

To commemorate the province of British Columbia's centennial in 1958, a summer series of performances by some of the world's great artists was established, with the idea that it would be presented annually. The Vancouver event was patterned on the famous Edinburgh Festival, inaugurated in 1947. Concerts, recitals, and productions took place throughout the city. (The Festival was abandoned within a few years: the price tag was considered far too high for a then-provincial city of just over a half-million people.)

New Canadian music was to be a token feature of the celebration, and the organizers commissioned Coulthard to write a work for a young Canadian singer beginning to make waves internationally. Coulthard, just back in Vancouver from a year in France, felt honoured by the request and determined to do her best in a new work for Maureen Forrester, soon to become Canada's greatest alto.

Looking for a theme, she remembered her father's devotion to poetry and chose texts by three of Canada's nineteenth-century Confederation Poets: Bliss Carman, W.E. Marshall, and Duncan Campbell Scott. To these she added a verse from the contemporary writer and one-time UBC colleague Louis MacKay, whose *Ill-Tempered Lover* she had come to know a few years earlier. All the poems feature nature metaphors and all mention some aspect of springtime. Coulthard decided to call the cycle *Spring Rhapsody.*

Spring Rhapsody is the vocal equivalent of a duo-sonata: the songs divide up into a fairly fast, expository first movement, a scherzo, slow movement, and finale. Some listeners may be content to take the work as a depiction of four different aspects of the season, but Coulthard's choice of texts — and, more significantly, their order in the cycle — allow and encourage a deeper interpretation.

"Now Great Orion Journeys to the West," the first song in the group, begins with brittle, icy piano figuration depicting winter's "glittering house" of ice and snow melting with the approach of spring. In contrast, the moment of spring is relaxed and pastoral until the intensity of growth and renewal (breathlessly pushed forward by elaborate keyboard figures, a transformed version of the opening materials) is interrupted by a climax that stops the song dead in its tracks.

"To a Mayflower" is coy and gentle. Coulthard remembered her father showing her mayflowers as a young girl on one of her first trips to eastern Canada. The period charm of the sonnet's language notwithstanding, its veiled eroticism continues the generative subtext of the cycle in no uncertain terms.

An unexpected darkness enters the cycle in its third section, "Admonition for Spring." The tempo is "dirge-like": tolling bells in the piano establish a processional mood as the poet reminds us of the impermanence of life and of beauty.

> See, in this wild green foam of growing things
> The heavy hyacinth remembering death.

A brief link passage (which Coulthard would quote decades later in her final composition for Forrester, *Four Prophetic Songs*) leads to "Ecstasy," a slightly abridged setting of a D.C. Scott poem comparing the work of an artist to the flight of a skylark. In Coulthard's first explicit evocation of the artist as mystic, the ecstasy of creation is expressed in music of surging intensity. Like the lark, the artist must produce, with or without an audience, with or without acclaim. "Heard or unheard in the night in the light/Sing there! Sing there!" is sung *majestico dramatico,* fused with keyboard figures

Babs and Jean picking mayflowers

from the opening song. A three-measure coda, incorporating bell-chords (from "Admonition for Spring") and a cadence of unambiguous finality, give the piano the last word.

The small audience who heard the premiere of *Spring Rhapsody* were moved by Maureen Forrester's and her long-time co-recitalist John Newmark's performance, but the work was not an immediate success. To help bring the composition to the attention of more performers and listeners, Coulthard allowed the final song to be published on its own. Canadian singers eventually came to know all four songs, finally published as a cycle in 1978. Coulthard also produced a version of the work for voice and small orchestra in 1963, but today the songs are best known, and certainly best loved, in their original format.

Jean Coulthard by Andreas Poulsson

5

A VOICE OF HER OWN

Coulthard's year in France confirmed to her that she was a Canadian and "professional" composer with a cosmopolitan accent and a traditional outlook. In the course of that winter in Paris and Roquebrune, she had made a start on an opera, sketched a violin concerto, written a draft of a piano quartet *(Sketches from a Medieval Town)*, and reasserted her connections to the music and musicians of Britain and Europe. She had been away from teaching and politics at UBC, and found herself at home in an artistic world beyond the Canadian musical community. The year in France reaffirmed her commitment as a composer and gave her the psychological strength to continue to grow as an artist.

> This period was a new lease on life for me, and I felt my independence from outside influences was again reaffirmed. In fact, I decided I didn't care at all what other people were writing or the fact that my means of musical expression were quite traditionally based. I

> realized that I had my own musical personality to develop and express. I've never intended to be a trailblazer, as some critics have ascertained, and I never will be one. It's just not my nature. (MWL)

When Coulthard returned to Vancouver, her daughter was about to enter high school. Her husband's business had become successful. Sister Babs offered strong moral support. Jean's professional ties with composers were occasionally helpful, and her links to the worlds of radio broadcasting and music publishing continued to expand. With a seemingly stable foundation in her private life, and with ongoing employment at UBC, Coulthard had freedom to make artistic choices.

Coulthard now knew exactly what she would do as a composer. She would continue to write in all the big forms of classical music: opera, concerti, symphonies, string quartets, and other chamber music — including a series of duo sonatas for all orchestral instruments. To this long list she added vocal, keyboard, and choral work. She would also compose "useful" work (the German term invented by Paul Hindemith is *Gebrauchsmusik*) for musical communities in Canada — children, students, amateurs, professional performers. And she would write more difficult music to stretch her own command of technique and expression.

Coulthard's productivity in the late 1950s and all through the 1960s was formidable. Whether or not her work was judged relevant by "new music" partisans, she had to write. Whether or not there was a commission or an audience, Coulthard was working — and on her own terms. Her biggest project was the three-act opera, *The Return of the Native,* begun in the back of a music store in Paris in 1955 and completed only in 1979. *The Return of the Native,* with its intricate plot of misalliance (and an intriguing autobiographical connection — Clem returns to Wessex from Paris to teach his provincial compatriots) is opera on its grandest scale. It requires a full complement of soloists, choir, and large orchestra. It is possibly the largest score on deposit at the Canadian Music Centre: four volumes and 548 pages of full-sized orchestral and vocal score. It took months of composing over several years merely to sketch the work, then a half-dozen winters in Hawaii to orchestrate fully. Its epic scale and psychological intensity, not to mention its huge cost in time and effort, showed stubborn commitment and massive perseverance — all of it work on a project that had not been commissioned and might never be performed.

Dozens of other works had similar histories. The lush, neoromantic *Piano Concerto* (1967), premiered by French pianist Marie-Aimée Varro in Ottawa, was never performed publicly again in Coulthard's lifetime. By contrast, *The Bird of Dawning Singeth All Night Long* (1960), for solo violin and small orchestra, became her most popular orchestral composition, recorded and broadcast again and again. The mammoth *Choral Symphony: "This Land"* (1967), a Centennial project for soloists, choir, and large orchestra, has yet to be performed. Her tough, Bartók-influenced *Second String Quartet* (1970), a threnody for the dead of World War II, was almost immediately recognized by chamber music aficionados as a major addition to the Canadian repertoire.

Her work slowly became better known to audiences of the BBC in Britain, the CBC in Canada, NBC, NPR, and CBS in the United States, France-Culture, the German and Austrian radio networks, and the Australian Broadcasting Commission. Her ever-increasing stature meant that Maureen Forrester would sing Coulthard's song cycles,[17] and that Coulthard works would be commissioned for festivals and artists from North America and Europe. Because work was commissioned and performed did not mean it was instantly understood or admired. Coulthard read press criticism with wry amusement, as her UBC archive shows. She would criticize the critics, penciling in surprisingly caustic comments when she thought a writer ill-prepared or uncomprehending.

Coulthard's "parallel career" at UBC continued. During the term, she found that teaching sometimes left her tired. There was the preparation of lectures, but then there was continuous correcting. Music theory can be a particularly marking-intensive discipline. Traditionally students are given extensive exercises in harmony, in counterpoint, or even in directed composition. That is all well and good in small seminars with a half-dozen students. UBC classes were double and triple that size. No matter, Coulthard continued to demand the same written work of her students. She would give assignments on the Friday so students could work through the weekend, leaving their teacher free to compose and to maintain her family life. But on Monday or Tuesday, when the assignments were handed in, she had to begin marking:

> I was correcting all week, apart from lectures, and then teaching composers separately. I remember before we got the music building [1967] we were in a little barn of a place. One day I went and there was no studio for me at all, so I taught in the car! (JC/WB, 2 February 1994)

Jean Coulthard thought her most important teaching work occurred in the 1960s and 1970s. Her composition pupils were mostly students in the Department of Music (after 1967, a full-fledged School of Music), but as she approached mandatory retirement, her private teaching grew apace. Eventually a group of talented young composers — Lloyd Burritt, Michael Baker, Chan Ka Nin, Jean Ethridge, Joan Hansen, Roger Knox, Sylvia Rickard, Frederick Schipizky, Ernst Schneider, among others — sought her out.[18] She was delighted to share her experience: the Wagenaar skills and the craft of orchestration and score preparation, not to mention practical advice on how to build a career.

It is difficult to attract the attention of a dispersed musical community like that in Canada and North America, and nearly impossible without help. Connections matter, all the more when they are broad, inclusive and diverse. Coulthard built on the old and solid foundation of friendships that began in the Vancouver elite of the 1920s, and extended through lifelong collaboration with musicians, artists, and poets, from every region of Canada and beyond. She occasionally acted as a concert promoter/fund-raiser, calling up her old Shaughnessy connections, inviting them to benefit concerts including new works by her students. "The ticket will be $10 if you come," she would cajole, "or $20 if you don't."

Through her teaching, she could recruit younger talents.

Coulthard teaching at UBC

Through her professional connections with publishers like Waterloo Music's Bill Brubacher or broadcasters like the CBC's Don Mowatt, she could pull strings.

These young composers wrote music in their own voices, gave mutual aid, and would continue to build on their earliest musical friendships with Coulthard. Coulthard now had the experience and the confidence to pass on to her students some hard-learned lessons. She had been around long enough to learn the fate of fads and bandwagons. She advised her students:

> If you are going to be a composer you have got to express yourself and nobody else. Somehow you have to find out what that is. I think young composers have to be influenced through certain phases — it's impossible not to be. But eventually you have to write exactly what you feel yourself. (JC/WB, 28 March 1996)

Thinking back to the difficulties of her own early years, Coulthard found practical ways to promote the new music of her students. The minute she judged a protégé was ready, a performance, broadcast,

The composers: Chan Ka Nin, Roger Knox, Jean Coulthard, Frederick Schipizky, Jean Ethridge, David Gordon Duke, Joan Hansen, Ernst Schneider, and Sylvia Rickard

or even publication was magically made possible. (Though she would deny it, Coulthard knew exactly how to use the cultural capital she had deposited over a lifetime. Now it was time to make withdrawals on behalf of her brood.) Composers studying with Coulthard went from the studio to the "real world" seemingly overnight.

Teaching composers was by no means Coulthard's only educational interest. Coulthard had come to believe a new audience for Canadian music could be built up from the thousands of young people taking lessons. Besides, pieces for learners were about the only publication consistently open to Canadian composers. Coulthard remembered her difficulties as a young teacher in finding good-quality teaching materials. In her theory teaching at UBC she recognized the problems of introducing what she habitually termed twentieth-century idioms to students. One of her most successful projects was a series of educational publications that launched former students Jean Ethridge, Sylvia Rickard, Joan Hansen, and David Gordon Duke. Ernst Schneider published teaching pieces on his own with his mentor's encouragement.

The network worked both ways. Often the massive task of copying and preparing scores was done partly by students. At various times, composers Michael Conway Baker and Frederick Schipizky orchestrated or adapted Coulthard works for the CBC Radio Orchestra.

The pattern of Coulthard's life was set by the late 1950s. She well understood that the day-to-day life of a composer is not a matter of waiting for inspiration (though she was happy when it came). Her profession demanded long hours and regular committed work. There was always at least one piece on the go: a commission, a piece for performer friends, or an addition to the ongoing sonata project. New ideas were worked out in yellow Conservatory Brand manuscript books — often begun, with a whiff of superstition, at the back page of each volume.[19] By this time even Coulthard's rough drafts reveal a professional command of technique. The books record changes and improvements, but large formal designs and overall direction are almost always clear. Good copies of works were then transcribed in soft pencil onto transparency sheets. Coulthard would re-write the entire composition on these sheets, then ink over the pencil draft to facilitate reproduction. Big works were usually sent off to a student assistant for inking. Finally, Coulthard would proofread for mistakes (never a task she was particularly good at), or make corrections.

Afternoons were for teaching at the University, late afternoons for tea and socializing with musicians and students, or attending to phone calls and letters. Coulthard's classes at UBC were formal in outline but highly idiosyncratic in content. Never a virtuoso lecturer, she was anxious that students understand theory in context: how major composers used idioms in significant works. She and her students studied compositions from the modern era in their entirety. Coulthard organized her teaching this way to show students what she called "form." Though she covered a broad range of materials and composers who mattered (whether she liked them or not), her lectures were filled with the subjective value judgments only a composer could make. An observant student could easily discover the touchstones of Coulthard's musical values, but also those transcendent moments — outside the boundaries of solid technique or fundamental craftsmanship — that elicited her admiration.

Coulthard's daughter Janey was embarking on her own professional training. She left Crofton House School for Girls, and took up a career as a painter. Jean and Don were pleased when Janey won a place at London's Chelsea School of Art and Design for 1961–1962. After that, she returned to the Vancouver School of Art in order to complete her certificate, graduating in 1965 with the Staff Scholarship — and then spent a final year back in London at the Slade School in 1965–1966.[20] With that, Jane Adams was off on a career of her own. As Coulthard's long-term plan for her own creative and professional career was starting to pay dividends, it was satisfying to see her daughter and her students productively launched on their artistic journeys.

After years of university teaching, Coulthard was still capable of cool self-criticism. Like her former teacher Ralph Vaughan Williams, Coulthard had nagging doubts about her prowess as an orchestral composer. On sabbatical leave in 1965–1966, Coulthard joined her daughter in London and took an entire academic term to attend the early music lectures of musicologist Thurston Dart, then professor at King's College, University of London. More importantly, she worked informally with the British composer and renowned orchestrator Gordon Jacob. Coulthard had long used Jacob's text *Orchestral Technique* with her students; armed with a written introduction from Elizabeth Poston, she took the train to Jacob's home in the near-London countryside. Later she said that before her studies with Jacob, she did not quite see the way to make powerful orchestral flourishes and climaxes, "to make orchestral music *build*." She brought with her the sketches for a tone poem, *Endymion*. Jacob showed her nuances of orchestral colour, and demonstrated how to pace her materials for maximum effect.

Coulthard's lessons with Jacob confirm that one is never too old to accept advice and insight. Her many trips to England and the Continent testify to her continual yearning to be part of the great

Gina Bachauer, dedicatee of the Aegean Sketches

European tradition, and led to such works as the piano quartet *Sketches from a Medieval Town* (the town being Roquebrune), *Music to St. Cecilia, Dopo Botticelli,* the *Six Medieval Love Songs,* and the *Aegean Sketches* for solo piano.

The *Aegean Sketches* (1961) were dedicated to Gina Bachauer, a Greek pianist whose international career ran from the early 1930s to the late 1960s. She played several times in Vancouver. Bachauer met Coulthard at a concert, and later accepted the dedication of the *Sketches.* The *Sketches* are condensed and persuasive musical references to the Greek world, an environment Coulthard came to know on a 1958 cruise through the Aegean. The showy pianistic

Sketches are attractive even on first hearing, but they repay close attention.

Consider *The Valley of the Butterflies,* the first of the three short pieces that make up the *Aegean Sketches.* It begins with quick, upward-moving broken chords, and melodic hints of the "near-eastern coast," for Turkey is just a few kilometres from the Valley of the Butterflies, and visible across the narrow strait. At about the halfway mark in the piece, we hear a rapid sequence of arpeggios — three notes against four, rising to the upper range of the piano — the fluttering movement of a million butterflies — in no way insistent, but spectacular. In the last page a few insects flutter away to the heights. Landscape was a regular source of "inspiration" for Coulthard.

The opening of "The Valley of the Butterflies"

In other works of the 1960s and 1970s, Coulthard began to define still more explicitly her sense of place in her native British Columbia.

> I have more than once ruminated on how to capture the mood and feeling of the West Coast in music. Arthur Benjamin encouraged me by saying that that the web of sound my works created suggested to him the feeling of the British Columbia coast. If one has been born in this land where earliest memories of life are walks in the woods, picnics in the bays and coves of its waters — summer vacations in the interior among the lakes and mountains — how could one (if at all sensitive to nature) fail to catch the atmosphere of this country? (MWL)

It was the late 1960s before Coulthard took up the legacy of British Columbia's pioneer artist, Emily Carr.[21] She had met the eccentric artist decades earlier when she and Don paid a visit to Carr's home in Victoria. As she recalls, it was at the end of the 1930s. She remembers how

> we intrepidly knocked on the front door and after waiting a little we decided no one was home. Then suddenly a high up window opened and Emily herself called down in a rather displeased voice (or so we thought), "Who is there?" We were a little taken aback — possibly by the extraordinary appearance of her dress. A gnome from the woods indeed. She wore on her head a comic little cap affair which was drawn tightly around her forehead with a black banding. . . . Once in her house, she couldn't have been more charming and our attack of trepidation soon vanished! She took us into the studio room where there were racks of her glorious paintings, I think she liked our youthful enthusiasm, for to the accompaniment of our excited "ohs!" and "ahs" she pulled out many for us to look at. As we commented some many years later, we could have had any one of the large oils for $50.00. But alas, young people with little to live on at the end of the depressed thirties had no extra money for another one. We counted ourselves very fortunate to own one. (PEC)

In old age Emily Carr began a second career as an author, producing several books of short stories and autobiographical sketches. Her diaries were published in 1966, long after her death, as *Hundreds and Thousands.* They show the struggles, the self-doubts, setbacks and, ultimately, the spiritual rewards of an artist's life.

Hundreds and Thousands resonated profoundly with Coulthard — the struggles of an artist deep in the West Coast landscape.

> The great artist Emily Carr lived to realize [the British Columbia coast] in her visual art, what about music? Perhaps it is harder to translate it into the most sophisticated of the arts. (MWL)

Coulthard fashioned a libretto for *The Pines of Emily Carr* out of excerpts from *Hundreds and Thousands,* and produced a score evoking the moods of the British Columbia coastal landscape and a meditation on an artist's life. She hoped to achieve in music what Carr had done in painting.[22]

By the late 1960s Coulthard had been composing for five

decades and her catalogue was extensive. It has long been fashionable to divide composers' output into periods or phases. As she looked back on her creative life (thus far), Coulthard preferred to see her music in two streams:

> Rather than dividing my music into periods as some composers do, I prefer to think of it being in two main streams of thought that have continuously run parallel to each other throughout my life. To develop this imagery: first, is the rippling lyrical nature of sunlight glinting on the watery stones of a small brook. The other is more brooding: the depth of one's being reflected in the deep fjords of our West Coast. In the first category I feel I have written many sunny and joyous works over the years: the *Fantasy* for violin, piano, and chamber orchestra, the *First String Quartet,* and my complete set of chamber duos for wind instruments and piano. The deeper, brooding works include the *Duo Sonata for Violin and Piano,* the *Second String Quartet* subtitled "Threnody," the *Variations on BACH* for piano, the *Octet: Twelve Essays on a Cantabile Theme,* and the *Symphonic Ode* for viola and orchestra. (MWL)

But many other classifications are possible. It is reasonable to pick out her travel pieces, her evocations of the British Columbia coast, her "northern" pieces — and to claim that these three groups show an increasing feeling for nature and the environment. We might distinguish these groups from her music about distant cultures, and her historically rooted works (the *Sketches from a Medieval Town* combines an appreciation of a distant culture with a feeling for travel and for history). Finally, there were works about personal, artistic, and spiritual growth.

THE MUSIC: *The Octet: Twelve Essays on a Cantabile Theme* (1972)

The *Octet: Twelve Essays on a Cantabile Theme* (1972) marks a high point in Coulthard's later career. Written at the end of her UBC years, it is both the logical outgrowth of her earlier work and a daring new venture exploring the contemporary musical language of the second half of the twentieth century.

The composition was intended for a CBC Vancouver Festival performance featuring the University of Alberta Quartet (led by Coulthard's long time friend and exponent Thomas Rolston) and the Vancouver-based Purcell String Quartet (with a similarly long and productive association with the composer). Given her familiarity with the players, Coulthard marked the score with their respective initials, using a practice she noticed in Vaughan Williams' *Serenade to Music.* She may well have conceived certain ideas with reference to the character and special musical gifts of the individual performers — the extroverted lyricism of favourite violinist Tom Rolston, the thoughtful warmth of cellist Ian Hampton.

The *Octet* is a personal re-definition of the variation idea: a single lode of concentrated motivic material is expanded and refined into twelve interlocking "essays." Four intertwined types of variations are featured in the work: slow and expressive, lyrical, scherzo-like and contrapuntal.

The *Cantabile Theme,* marked *Lento pensivo,* is presented twice, an initial statement in one quartet answered by an inverted version in the other quartet, and is structured along quasi-fugal lines. The theme itself comprises four significant melodic cells:

a) a rising motive of major second, minor second, fourth, and fifth
b) a descending minor second and minor third figure, identical to a cell used in the second of the *Two Night Songs* for baritone, piano and string quartet
c) an undulating figure of ascending and descending seconds
d) a descending chromatic figure followed by a descending leap.

The first essay, *Motivation,* redistributes the two quartets into a string ensemble format, extending the previously cryptic theme elements into more expansive melodic lines presented over a "motivationally" pulsing rhythmic accompaniment in compound triple time.

Visionary Song, marked *Adagio cantabile espressivo,* returns to the spirit of the opening. The predominating mood is quiet and lyrical, then the coda establishes a portentous *misterioso* mood that propels the music into the first of three scherzos.

Turbulence is a robust *Allegro con brio* scherzo characterized by motoristic 16th- note figures and dramatic *glissandi.*

As the movement builds in intensity, the phrase length is severely truncated, with interrupted climactic ejaculations (measures 17–20), before subsiding back to the slow *misterioso* mood of the previous link passage.

Summer Night on the Water fuses the legato lyricism of the theme and the visionary song with the pulsing motivational triplets of the second essay to create a languid and watery mood piece for string ensemble.

Echoes triggers a set of movements characterized above all by a contrapuntal interplay that shows the equal importance of both string quartets and all eight players.

The Academicians, Chimera, and *Transfiguration* form the core of the work. *The Academicians,* a series of grotesque canons, injects a note of irony—a rare instance of Coulthard exploring overt (if embittered) satire. The *Octet* was conceived just prior to Coulthard's retirement from the University of British Columbia. *The Academicians* is a salute to her colleagues, a depiction of a faculty meeting—with "the voice of one particular colleague becoming higher and squeakier" as the acrimony intensifies.

Chimera is the second of the composition's three scherzos and uses Coulthard's most extreme exploration of string effects. These include harmonics, regular and *ponticello pizzicato, tremolo,* and microtones.

Transfiguration marks the central, lyric keystone of the work, linking the opening mood of expectant lyricism to the resigned but ineffably beautiful *Farewell.*

The Wood Doves Grieve was written to evoke the gentle spirit of the late Clementine Poston (mother of Coulthard's British composer friend Elizabeth Poston). The eponymous doves were residents in the gardens and woodlands surrounding the Postons' home, E.M. Forster's "Howard's End."

Clementine Poston by Joy Finzi

Fugue is the climax of the contrapuntal stream of organization in the composition, the developmental outgrowth of the *Theme, Echoes,* and *The Academicians.* The fugue subject uses a rhythm from J.S. Bach and recalls Coulthard's other Bach-inspired works: Coulthard has designed an especially ingenious tonal scheme presenting the subject transposed on all twelve tones accessed through the cycle of fifths (a plan indebted to Bartók's opening movement in *Music for strings, percussion, and celesta,* but decidedly un-Bartókian in effect).

Night Wind, a reference to the classical metaphor for inspiration, is the last of the three scherzo movements, and is rondo-like in structure.

In the final essay, *Farewell,* Coulthard returns to the concentrated lyricism of the opening, establishing a mood of great beauty touched with resignation. *Farewell* is in every sense the culmination of the essays but, characteristically, offers an enigmatic and pensive ending, not a grand, massive finale.

The final essays recapitulate and rework ideas from earlier segments. Thus *The Wood Doves Grieve* is a linking of contrapuntal and lyric elements. The *Fugue* is the culmination of the contrapuntal variations, while *Night Wind* fuses lyric and scherzo elements. In this way the form reads, on one level, as a free arch, on another as an exposition, development, and recapitulation.

What was in Coulthard's mind? Since her work with Bernard Wagenaar, Coulthard had set herself challenges: writing in major forms, writing string quartets, writing an extended dramatic work. The string octet repertoire is slight, with works by Spohr, a composer in whom Coulthard had no particular interest, Mendelssohn, and the interlocking quartets of Coulthard's one-time teacher Milhaud. Although Coulthard thought that some of the movements of the *Octet* were almost orchestral, the great challenge was to write a major work for large ensemble that preserved the independence of expression of good chamber writing for all instruments.

Beyond the obvious challenge, and the equally obvious pleasure of writing for a collection of highly regarded professional and personal friends, it is impossible not to notice the work was produced during the year Coulthard prepared for retirement from UBC. The 1960s and early 1970s were double-edged for Coulthard: on one hand she was regularly told that her more lyrical work was irrelevant and outdated; on the other, performers more frequently sought her out and there was revived interest in her music. Coulthard meant the *Octet* as a measure of her stature as an artist and a statement of individuality. It does encompass farewells — to friends, her colleagues, to the idea of her parallel career. But it also maps out a rich and unimaginably productive future: almost two further decades of ecstatic music making and seventy-eight entirely new works.

Jean Coulthard by Andreas Poulsson

6

AT LAST, A TIME FOR MUSIC

Her sixty-fifth birthday in 1973 forced Coulthard to retire from university teaching. As far as most of the UBC faculty — predominantly male, overwhelmingly American or American-trained — was concerned, her retirement was long overdue. Although Coulthard had on balance enjoyed her UBC employment, she had been marginalized.

Her marginality is surprising, considering her steadily increasing stature and visibility in Canada and abroad in the 1960s and early 1970s. But Coulthard's academic marginality was partly *caused* by her growing reputation as a composer.[23] Mass recruitment of American-trained and American-born professors between 1958 and 1965 transformed the UBC music department. With these hirings came an extensive overhaul of the UBC curriculum to include additional courses in music theory, music history, composition, as well as ensemble and individual instruction in voice and instruments.

The UBC model derived from the curricula of Eastman, Juilliard, and the University of Southern California (USC) after the hiring of G. Welton Marquis as Head of Department in 1957. Marquis recruited an extensive cadre of USC-trained professors who remade Adaskin's amateur department into a full-scale School of Music resolutely consistent with American models.

Coulthard, as a Canadian-born artist with English and European experience, retreated into the woodwork. She was sometimes grudgingly respected, at other times invisible. Coulthard's circumstances were not exceptional, as these were ambiguous times for women in university music departments. Practical teachers, especially women with reputations as pianists and singers, were regularly recruited; on the other hand, senior academics and administrators were nearly always men. Coulthard was a caring teacher, working at a time when male administrators and senior academics held all the cards. UBC rarely noticed her when it made decisions about curriculum, salary, or other scholarly benefits.

For UBC's new academics, publish-or-perish was becoming the rallying cry of the day. Coulthard might publish her music, but she was no scholar or researcher. Among so many American or American-trained faculty members, Coulthard's enthusiasm for all things Canadian was thought "quaint." She had reason to move on to the next phase of her creative life.

She had enjoyed her students, had found it professionally useful to be a university lecturer, had retained a fondness for the Library and the Faculty Club, and had the quiet satisfaction of using every spare moment in summers and sabbaticals to write music. "Retirement" gave her redoubled opportunity for concentrated work.

If the compositional establishment thought Coulthard's work hopelessly old-fashioned, she had nonetheless moved far along a path of her own choosing and acquired firm confidence in her style. Now that she was out on her own, her immediate practical task was to find effective strategies to build her reputation.

Only a few composers in the 1960s and 1970s thought it worthwhile to write educational music, concentrating instead on commissions for burgeoning new music competitions, specialist broadcasting, and electro-acoustic experiments. Coulthard disagreed. One way she kept her work in the public eye was by writing and publishing for students. Years of teaching in her mother's studio had given her a strongly practical idea of what young performers needed to play — and what they might *want* to play. Good-quality materials remained hard to come by. The only type of publication consistently profitable for Canadian publishers and composers was educational music.

> I was asked by William Brubacher of the Waterloo Music Company to write a comprehensive series of graded piano books. I invited two of my composer students to join me in this exciting project. And my daughter the painter, Jane Adams, did all the illustrations and cover designs. From then on I dubbed this series "a family affair." Our books were especially designed to be of help to younger teachers working on their own. There now are eleven books entitled *Music of Our Time* in print, and you can well understand it was a great undertaking to try and introduce each 20th century idiom into the series step by step and to integrate all in a proper sequence for students. (MWL)

The educational aspect of her work occupied more time and more pages after 1973 than before. Coulthard, working with various publishers, would create over the next fifteen years one of the largest bodies of educational works yet published in Canada. Perhaps the best known of the teaching series are *Music of Our Time* for piano, *A la Jeunesse* (later re-titled *The Encore Series*) for violin, *Earth Music* for cello, and significant other repertoire for keyboard, voice, choirs, and ensembles.

A cover by Janey

Remembering her work as a teacher, Coulthard never allowed her educational music to be self-indulgent: pieces had to have a teaching point — an aspect of twentieth-century harmony, an idea

L-R: Corey and Katja Cerovsek with Jean, Babs, and Don, 1981

about formal organization, an etude designed to stretch a performer's expressive, technical, or imaginative powers. Coulthard made detailed studies of standard pedagogical works, always aware that teachers would reject pieces, however good, that did not conform to solid pedagogical precedent. A number of Coulthard works became minor classics, thus bringing her name to generations of Canadian children. From the 1970s on a year rarely passed without additions to what she called her junior catalogue.

Part of her post-retirement routine was to help teachers and their students in workshops and festivals. Young performers were too often terrified by the thought of playing their pieces for "the composer." Coulthard had years of practical experience and knew how to bring out the best in her young interpreters. Through her junior catalogue, and performances of it, she met up-and-coming performers Jon Kimura Parker, Katja and Corey Cerovsek, Gwen and Desmond Hoebig — to name just a few — when they were very young.

Moreover, even into her eighties Coulthard received commissions and requests from groups such as the Toronto Children's Choir, the Canadian Music Competition, and the Vancouver Academy of Music.

Although the proportions of her output changed after 1973, Coulthard retained her strong commitment to the creation of concert music. Compositions in the tradition of her *Octet* showed Coulthard at her most personal and intellectual. Other works targeted a broader audience: people still sceptical of "new music" who had to be coaxed along. Coulthard's orchestral suite *Canada Mosaic* tried to reach as many listeners as possible, while containing music full of conviction.

After her retirement from UBC, Coulthard continued to teach professional-level students, necessarily at home. Lessons were always rigorous, but when the hard work was over, sessions spilt over into afternoon tea or even sherry, and good conversation about music, the arts, and travel. Coulthard's students received a sense of perspective, not just the tools of their trade.

She branched out into new sub-careers. She took an interest in music festivals and in broadcasting, sometimes combining the two. Coulthard believed that in a country like Canada, culturally complicated and sparsely populated, it was irresponsible to hide in one's studio and just write music. Even with the enthusiastic support of former students, and the distribution of her educational works, she wanted to find more ways to keep her music before the public. Artists sometimes have to *create* their own organizations. Painters find themselves helping to found art galleries or fund them. Poets launch publishing houses. Musicians create festivals and radio series, participate in governing the Canadian Music Centre, work together in the Canadian League of Composers, speak in support of the Canada Council, and much else. Coulthard realized that

> whereas in the past composers were sustained by wealthy patrons and the church, today they rely on commissions from federal funding sources, provincial supporting bodies, and special endowments. (EC)

Coulthard had developed a political idea of the arts. Although she would never have drawn attention to this, she had all along been developing a new social classification — that of a busy professional composer working in the Canadian West. When she was born, there "simply weren't any composers to speak of in Vancouver."[24]

An important speech delivered at the Banff Centre outlined the life and responsibilities of "The Eclectic Composer of Today"[25] — really describing her own life as a composer and her own sense of responsibility to art and to her audience. Coulthard thought composers working in a Canadian environment should divide their output, writing not just "ivory tower" works for personal aesthetic satisfaction — but working as generalists prepared to write for children, for favoured performers, for community ensembles, film and television, and for career-building competition.

Coulthard's husband Don Adams had likewise been caught up in the idea of building a new professional role. Jean commented that

> Don wasn't a painter or anything like that, but he had a great artistic vision in all things, including music. He could play the piano quite well — or would have, if he'd practiced! When Don finally got his business established, it was a means of developing his whole nature. He did beautiful things in that shop, which was more like a gallery than a shop. He used to hold formal art exhibits, and arrange art lectures. (JC/WB, 6 April 1994)

His atelier, Don Adams Interiors, set a new standard for design in Vancouver, and his eclectic style, which mixed Scandinavian, Spanish, Mexican, and Asian materials and motifs, became extremely influential. As Coulthard entered her "retirement" of fresh activism, her now-retired husband began to think about his own life as an artist, interior designer, and businessman. Don had developed his own ideas about how to live "a designed life," reinvigorating the Arts-and-Crafts principles of his youth to suit the affluent closing decades of the twentieth century. Eclecticism came as naturally to Don as it did to Jean; his credo was expressed in an unpublished book-length manuscript, "A Place to Hang Your Hat," and in lectures and classes for would-be designers.[26]

The Coulthard/Adams home had been a base of operations, not just the "secret place of the heart" where high art was conceived and made. The house on Vancouver's South West Marine Drive was a showcase and a testing laboratory for Adams. Coulthard said it was exasperating to become fond of a chair or table only to come home to find it sold and replaced. Coulthard's personal style was more traditional, and her neoclassical desk, antique chairs, and accents provided unexpected grace notes to the sophisticated "Adams style."

Jean and Don both liked to entertain. Work came first, but there was always time for parties and receptions. Coulthard had learned to use entertainment as a gracious if subtle form of self-promotion. Where a male composer might meet musician friends over post-concert drinks, Coulthard invited guests to her home. Honoured celebrities might include Glenn Gould, John Ogdon, Maureen Forrester, Evelyn and John Barbirolli, or Tom Rolston and Isobel

The Don Adams style at 2747 South West Marine Drive

Jean, Jane, and Don at home

Moore. These gatherings usually started with tea in Coulthard's large Japanese-flavoured music room, moved on to the formal living room for drinks, and, when the weather was good, moved out into the manicured gardens and terraces that surrounded the house. Visitors left believing they had glimpsed a true West Coast lifestyle.

If the house was mostly Don's preserve, both Don and Jean were devoted gardeners. Don occupied himself with form and detail, Jean was more sentimentally interested in favoured flowers, and would say that the nature titles in her work often had their first inspiration right at home.

Don and Jean took up the habit of winter vacations in Hawaii. With the help of an old Vancouver musical friend, they found a garden house in Honolulu for low rent. As Don's business interests tapered off, these trips lengthened to two, then three months. For most winters between 1973 and 1983, they lived a happily sedentary existence just east of Diamond Head, Honolulu's ancient landmark. Don flatly refused little excursions and side-trips, happy to

The garden at 2747 Marine Drive

stay in the garden or on the beach. Jean was more active. Their landlord was a likeable medical man, Ralph Cloward, who commented in 1995:

> [T]hey'd come every winter and stay for four or five months or longer. Very, very lovely people. Because I was an amateur musician, I was interested in her. But I found she didn't *play* music, she invented it! So she would rent a small piano and they would bring it down here and put it in the cottage, and she'd spend her days sitting there, playing chords on this little piano. All I'd hear would be one or two notes or a few chords, and that's all that came out of it, but she was busy putting it down on paper. And then she'd take a big symphony back to Canada. (RC/WB January 1995)

Don and Jean in the garden

THE MUSIC: *Canada Mosaic* (1974)

Canada Mosaic was composed at a key moment of Canadian cultural development. The early 1970s were a time for Canada to assert its identity. The very successful Expo '67 was over and the nation was reconsidering its identity and its culture. Beyond our borders, few changes were more significant than the establishment of official relations with China.

In 1973 the Vancouver Symphony Orchestra was asked to perform in the People's Republic of China. The political authorities in China were highly specific about the sort of music the orchestra could play. Although they wanted a new work by a Canadian composer, the authorities required "music of the people", not in a difficult, dissonant, or "avant-garde" style.

When the VSO approached Coulthard, she at first saw the assignment as a back-handed compliment and did not know what to do faced with this recipe for music. She disliked the idea of anyone dictating what she could or could not write, and thought it ludicrous to imagine thousands of Canadians singing folk songs as they worked. But Coulthard had always liked writing music for the general audience. She liked folk songs and, in the end, she also liked to think that the commission might promote understanding between two countries.

In far-off Hawaii, Coulthard decided to write a work for large orchestra based on folk songs from all regions of Canada. To justify using this uncomplicated music, she framed the orchestral folk songs with two memories from her own childhood: the opening *Lullaby for a Snowy Night* and the concluding *New Year's Celebration.*

The interior movements are considerably more than song settings and harmonizations. Coulthard creates miniature fantasies on folk materials: original compositions in brilliant orchestral style, forming a "mosaic" built out of fragments of songs and traditional music.

Mam'zelle Québécoise is a waltz derived from the little-known French Canadian folk song *La belle Françoise.* Sleigh bells at the end make the connection with the opening *Lullaby.*

Coulthard's own British Columbia coast is represented by two movements: *D'Sonoqua's Song* describes the famous painting and short story by Emily Carr. Coulthard knew from the pioneer ethnomusicologist and expert on First Nations music Ida Halpern that hereditary music was owned by its singer-songmakers. Coulthard felt she could use formulas and rhythms but, quite consciously, did not quote an entire song.

Harbour Sounds is a passacaglia with variations based on a Franco-Ontarian song from the Ottawa Valley, *V'la bon vent.*

The Contented House is based on the well-known folk melody *A la claire fontaine.* Here Coulthard makes another reference to her

Emily Carr, Zunoqua of the Cat Village, *1931*
oil on canvas, 112.2 x 70.1 cm, Vancouver Art Gallery, VAG 42.3.21 (Photo: Trevor Mills)

childhood. She remembered her father telling her that the tune was a favourite of Canada's first Prime Minister, Sir John A. Macdonald.

Next is *Billowing Fields of Golden Wheat,* a setting of a Ukrainian melody from the prairies, one of only a handful of orchestral works that use songs from this important group of settlers in the Canadian West.

The work ends with a loud and exuberant depiction of Vancouver's Chinese New Year: lion dances, lots of firecrackers (played by two whips in the percussion section) and, unexpectedly, a last quotation from an early Coulthard work, a theme from her 1948 choral piece *Quebec May,* here given to the brass.

Jean Coulthard with Alexa and Janey, Montreal, 1978

Coulthard worked hard and fast on the composition, which was ready for rehearsal long before the projected tour. Unfortunately, almost nothing went as planned. Conditions changed rapidly in China and the invitation was withdrawn. *Canada Mosaic* ended up having its first unofficial performance in Vancouver, then receiving an official premiere in Japan where the orchestra toured with conductor Kazyoshi Akiyama in 1974.

Although *Canada Mosaic* is not an especially long orchestral suite, it is for very large orchestra. Akiyama specifically asked that it have short solos for most of the VSO members (so that everyone could go on the tour). For a number of years the size of orchestra required prevented regular performances until CBC producer (and former student) George Laverock suggested that Coulthard arrange a few movements for smaller forces. The resulting *Introduction and Three Folk Songs* (from *Canada Mosaic*) was recorded by the CBC Radio Orchestra and is frequently heard today.

Jean Coulthard illustrating a musical point with granddaughter Alexa

Just before Coulthard left UBC, her daughter Jane Adams, now a professional artist, married cinematographer and photographer Andreas Poulsson. The young couple moved to Montreal, where Andreas pursued a career with the National Film Board and Jane continued hers as a painter and print-maker.

Jean visited her daughter and son-in-law in Montreal two and even three times a year, especially after the birth of her granddaughter Alexa in 1975. Once again Coulthard rented a small upright piano for her improvised studio in her daughter's Westmount home so she could work during her visits. As the author of any number of grandmother pieces, most published in *Music of Our Time,* Coulthard proved an active, working grandparent.

Canada's musical centres are often insular if not self-contained. After her retirement, Coulthard expanded her network to include faithful musical friends in Quebec. Violist Robert Verebes, of the Montreal Symphony Orchestra, having learned and played Coulthard's *Sonata Rhapsody* for viola and piano (1962), wanted a concerto. He then commissioned the *Symphonic Ode* for viola and orchestra. Clarinetist Sherman Friedland of Concordia University asked her to write *Shelley Portrait* in 1987. Broadcaster Monique Grenier and *Le Devoir* critic Gilles Potvin were involved in projects. Ross Pratt, one of Canada's best-known pianists and teachers in the second half of the twentieth century, was a Montrealer. Pratt taught at London's Royal Academy of Music from time to time, and did much for Canadian music. It was Pratt who frequently performed and first recorded Coulthard's 1st and 2nd *Etudes* for the CBC, and it is worth noting that Coulthard's music was more and more often connected in the same programs to works by her western compatriots Violet Archer and Barbara Pentland.

Daughter Janey now played an active part in her mother's career. To try to drum up interest in a staging of *The Return of the Native,* Janey was enlisted to draw sample costume designs and sets to give a feeling for how a complete production might look. In addition, Jane's art work made Coulthard's educational projects and individual compositions visually attractive.

The Return of the Native

It began to look as though Coulthard would continue her artistic career until she could no longer lift a pencil. She actively kept up her trans-Atlantic network of professional friends. English composer (by then Master of the Queen's Music) Sir Arthur Bliss and his California-born wife Trudy became important friends. As part of her campaign to promote her music, and Canadian music in general, she made a point of attending performances wherever they might occur. That meant trips back to England and France — as for example, when the University of Alberta String Quartet, led by Tom Rolston, performed her *Second String Quartet.*

> Arthur Bliss was president of the Cheltenham Festival and was thrilled with my *Second String Quartet,* one of my best, I think. I wrote it for the University of Alberta Quartet. We all went to the Cheltenham Festival and had a wonderful time there, as you can imagine. (JC/WB, 6 April 1994)

Connections bred connections. Coulthard tagged along with Arthur Bliss and his wife in a visit to Benjamin Britten's famous Aldeburgh Festival. There she met not only Britten and tenor Peter Pears, but their great friends Mstislav Rostropovich and his soprano wife Galina Vishnevskaya. To Bliss's amusement, Coulthard and the diva disagreed over politics — with Coulthard in the unexpected position of defending American ways to uncomprehending Europeans.

Jean Coulthard, Mstislav Rostropovich, Sir Arthur Bliss, unidentified person, and Galina Vishnevskaya at Aldeburgh

Within Canada, she was regularly travelling to hear premieres or to supervise recordings. She found herself giving talks at conferences. For someone who enjoyed travelling anyway, these experiences were a reward for hard work over many decades.

On her seventieth and eightieth birthdays she received significant honours — recognition from teacher and professional groups, honorary doctorates from UBC and Concordia, and the Orders of Canada and of British Columbia.[27] In turn, through celebratory performances and broadcasts and publications, the Canadian musical public became more aware of Coulthard's art. One of the grandest occasions was a seventieth-birthday concert in Vancouver's Playhouse Theatre. Ostensibly a benefit for the Vancouver Women's Musical Club Scholarship Fund, an organization Coulthard's mother helped found at the turn of the century, the concert brought together a cross-section of Coulthard's favourite performers: Maureen Forrester, Thomas Rolston, Ross Pratt, and John Newmark. The Playhouse was normally devoted to live theatre, and an elegant theatrical set was already in place. Husband Don imported "half the garden" from 2747 Marine Drive to make the stage more attractive.

Rehearsals were intense: lots of musicians, little time, tremendously demanding music. Even the great Maureen Forrester couldn't resist pointing out how exacting a composer Coulthard could be. In the third of the *Spring Rhapsody* songs, Forrester sang the line, "The heavy hyacinth . . ." in her trademark golden alto voice — then without missing a beat, interjected "Lousy word, Jean!" — before completing the phrase ". . . remembers death." The Vancouver audience knew Coulthard was one of their own, but many of the almost seven hundred listeners were not a little surprised by the scope and depth of the evening-long concert.

Arts festivals had become a Canadian tradition. Strong in most regions, they became an important aspect of cultural life after the war. In the early 1970s, visionary Alys Monod was convinced that something must be done to promote music in British Columbia's Okanagan region. She knew of Coulthard as B.C.'s senior com-

At Cheltenham with the University of Alberta String Quartet

Seventieth-birthday concert with John Newmark and Maureen Forrester

poser, and a productive working and personal relationship ensued. They chose the Okanagan because it is roughly halfway between British Columbia's coast and Alberta's major cities, and they wanted to include both Alberta and B.C. musicians. Coulthard believed the festival should be special and different. She imagined a place for young composers to meet, hear their works performed and adjudicated by senior composers, exchange ideas, and form bonds. Using the facilities of holiday camps in the Thompson/Okanagan region, the festival took place in late May (just at the height of the local asparagus season, as Coulthard joked). Performers were brought in from the larger centres, adjudicators (including Violet Archer from Edmonton, Richard Johnston from Calgary, Oskar Morawetz from Toronto, and Gilles Tremblay from Montreal) were cajoled into attending. Dozens of composers submitted scores and came for performances.

Other booming arts programs, well away from large urban centres, were attractive to Coulthard, who never missed an opportunity to seek renewal in western Canada's natural surroundings. She was connected with two organizations on Vancouver Island: the Shawnigan Summer School of the Arts and the summer programs of the Victoria Conservatory. At J. J. Johannesen's Shawnigan School, no provisions had been made for performances of new compositions. Coulthard mobilized her brood and a weekly New Music Series was quickly arranged. Everyone contributed to a fund to provide a "nice glass of sherry" for performers, composers, and audiences. The concerts were a runaway success. Both Vancouver Island programs allowed her to continue with teaching and mentoring, but were far less time-intensive than her previous teaching at UBC.

Then there was Banff. The Banff Centre for the Arts was set up in 1933, but the Centre's music programs became especially influential in the early 1970s under the leadership of Coulthard's old friends Thomas Rolston and Isobel Moore.

Coulthard adored the Rolstons. Her connection to them was easily one of her most long-standing personal and professional friendships. She coached the *Duo Sonata* (1952) with Tom and Isobel in the 1950s, revised her expansive *Violin Concerto* (1959) with Tom, composed numerous piano-and-violin works, even going so far as to write a piano-and-harp composition for the pair when Isobel took up that instrument. Coulthard went on to create pieces for their famous cellist daughter, Shauna. Two of Coulthard's late works were Rolston-inspired, the *Sonata* for solo violin (1979) for Tom himself, as a last gift, and the extraordinary *Sonata* for violin and cello (1989) for Tom and Shauna.

When Tom and Isobel contacted Coulthard to ask if she might like to join the Centre for at least a summer or two, her decision must have been relatively easy. She visited Banff in 1976 to consult about the Centre's plans to establish composer programs, then taught at the Centre in 1978 and 1979. Her own grand piano now resides there. In Banff and the Okanagan, Coulthard established or renewed friendships with compositional colleagues — among them Poland's Witold Lutosłavsky, American William Schuman (a former Wagenaar pupil), and Canadian composers Oscar Morawetz, Serge Garant, and in particular Violet Archer, in first-rate concerts, small seminars, impromptu discussions, and lots of happy picnics in the woods.

Western Canada was home to Jean Coulthard, Barbara Pentland, and Violet Archer, a trio of powerful composers who happened to be women. It was ironic that the public took heightened notice of these women's lives and work only after their deaths, all in a six-week period in 2000. But it would be wrong to exaggerate. None of the three was unknown. These women's musical output had attracted substantial support *during* their careers. It will not do to say that theirs was hard, pioneering work, completely unrecognized until their deaths. As is so often the case, the truth lies somewhere between the two extremes. Take the case of Violet Archer.

Like Coulthard, Violet Archer intensified her educational and compositional work after retirement in 1978. Archer, too, played a part in the development of the Banff Centre, the Canadian Music Centre, and the Canada Council. In each of these fields, Archer worked to ensure that her favoured institutions would live on after her death to bring Canadian music into as many lives and living rooms as possible.

Coulthard, Archer, and Pentland were late bloomers. These composers took time to grow and to mature before they attempted their greatest work. Coulthard was nearly forty years old when her first great sequence of sonatas and chambers works appeared. Pentland acquired her mature voice after study in Darmstadt, Germany, in the 1950s. Archer's career took off after her return to Canada in 1960.

But some late bloomers then contrive to bloom for a long time. Coulthard's most productive period was the long and intensive sequence of creation begun after age sixty-five. Archer was similarly productive until the very end of her life. Until Pentland's lengthy illness in the 1990s, she too maintained a committed musical life.[28]

As Coulthard approached her ninth decade she could look back on years of concentrated, serious work. Despite a slow start, her fifties, sixties, and seventies saw the production of a rich and varied portfolio of work in all genres. She had helped to teach a new generation of composers and tried to animate the public's interest in Canadian new music.

Coulthard's work came to form a part of the Canadian musical heritage. Not many composers live to see their works go in, and out, and back in the revolving door of musical fashion. Coulthard lived to see her music firmly set in the nation's artistic fabric.

With Jane, by Andreas Poulsson

7

FAREWELL

In her seventies Coulthard told a composition student she would be perfectly happy to compose until she was eighty, then *really* retire. But as her eightieth birthday approached, composition proved too much an ingrained way of life for Coulthard to give it up. Her personal circumstances were such that it might have made sense to ease up on her creative work. By the early 1980s, the house at 2747 Marine Drive in Vancouver was too big and the garden too extensive for a couple in their seventies. The solution was to sell up and move. In 1983 Don and Jean chose a town house in West Vancouver, the most coastal in feeling of the Vancouver suburbs. Jean's sister, Babs, had long lived in a beachfront home in West Vancouver, and Jean's nephews lived in the neighbourhood. Don and Jean now found a building just steps away from picturesque Caulfeild Cove. It was an easy drive to Babs's place, cold swims on her private beach and restorative cups of tea.

Don Adams did not have many years in West Vancouver. He had found a happy niche as a part-time lecturer on interior design. His success was considerable, and a Don Adams IDI (Interior Design) scholarship at suburban Kwantlen College commemorates his work.[29] Don enjoyed his teaching work as Jean had enjoyed hers. But otherwise, Don found it hard to adjust to the 1980s. He disliked the "glitz" of the period and thought that style and elegance were vanishing from life. He considered various ways of sharing his entrepreneurial experience with Third World cadres, but nothing came of it. He died in 1985 of a heart attack. More than ever, Jean Coulthard appreciated living near her sister Babs. Always close, the sisters were now in daily contact.

Coulthard had not thought what a composer in extreme old age might — or should — do. But, as she had done all through her career, she made sense of her life by composing. Although the *Autumn Symphony* is on the surface abstract concert music, anyone closely considering Coulthard's last symphony cannot avoid its autobiographical and philosophical bent. It is a work that could be written only by a composer in the autumn of her career. Other works such as the *Sonata* for violin and cello and *Image Terrestre,* would not have been written at an earlier stage in her life. Her late work referenced people, places, emotions, and philosophies that she understood in the prism of maturity.

Considering her priorities, she began to scale back her public activities. Problems with eyesight made long works for large orchestra impractical. Still she wrote.

Just as the circumstances of Coulthard's life swiftly changed in the 1980s, so did her city's. Vancouver at the end of the twentieth century would have been unimaginable to the pioneers of one hundred years earlier. With a population of over two million in a densely inhabited downtown and sprawling suburbs, it had become a Pacific Rim city as strongly linked to Hong Kong/Tokyo/Taipei as to San Francisco/Los Angeles.

Some elements were unchanged: Vancouverites still loved their gardens and their boats, still boasted about their wonderful climate

Vancouver at the end of the 20th century

(while privately grumbling about dark winter days and year-round rain), still looked to the big cities of Europe and the United States for culture — and still had chips on their shoulders about Eastern Canada (now called Central Canada, but still meaning Toronto).

Vancouver thought of itself as a musical centre claiming North American significance. But as late as the late 1970s, it had been inconvenient and even discouraging for Coulthard (and artists in most fields) to build a career on a Vancouver base. By the turn of the millennium, in music, painting, architecture, design, dance, and more, the continent had begun to take notice of Vancouver artists.

For long years Coulthard's own survival technique had been simple. She was more interested in the next piece than the last one.

That attitude was enough to keep her working optimistically, even when she felt isolated, if not neglected. In her final decade, she took care to finish long-term projects. Her opera *The Return of the Native,* begun in the mid-'50s, was completed in a full-length orchestral version in 1979. Perhaps recalling Hindemith's symphonies taken from his *Mathis der Maler* (1934) and *Die Harmonie der Welt* (1951), Coulthard created more practical adaptations of the music, including the choral suite *When Tempests Rise.* The suite had concert readings in 1987, and a piano/vocal version of the complete opera was produced by Bliss Johnston in a run at the Vancouver Academy of Music in September 1993.

Coulthard then completed her sonata series, begun in the late 1940s, with new ones for trumpet and piano, and french horn and piano. She joked that she could not warm to the notion of trombone and double bass works. She "cheated" by writing a longish one-movement "rondelay" for harp, *Of Fields and Forests,* in modified sonata form.

She revised and adapted a number of compositions written at earlier stages of her career. The *Serenade* for strings of 1961 was revised in 1988 at the request of Robert Verebes for viola with string accompaniment. She divided the orchestration of *Quebec May* with former student Frederick Schipizky. Another former student, successful film and television composer Michael Conway Baker, orchestrated a selection of his former teacher's *Six Irish Poems.*

Any number of composers have done this sort of thing, especially toward the ends of their careers. It is helpful to musicians, audiences, and students when composers make their works more playable on more and different instruments, and in more and different ways. It was telling that Coulthard's last twenty-five years of creative interest combined two types of writing: *re*-writing of older works, and the creation of whole new sequences of works.

For example, excepting *A la Jeunesse,* her third sonata for violin and piano, Coulthard considered her series of duo sonatas finished. In their place, she conceived a new project — descriptive suites for her favourite instruments and/or performers. Among these were *Dopo Botticelli* for cello and piano, *Where The Trade Winds Blow* for flute and piano, *Frescoes* for violin and harp, and *Gardens* for clarinet and piano. There were new works for strings *without* piano, sonatas for solo violin, guitar, and violin and cello. Her final completed work was a sonata for solo cello.

> Brian Mix reminded me that I'd done a cello sonata, and a cello piece to be done with strings and various other cello things, but I had never written a solo cello sonatina or a sonata. So we decided that I should do that next. I just was thinking about what would be necessary to have a substantial work for solo cello, much harder than having a nice piano to fill in places. And it's quite difficult if you're not a cellist. It either comes or it doesn't. Some days it doesn't work. It's a funny business, isn't it, the creative process? (JC/WB, 22 January 1994)

Ecological concern motivated three pieces: *Image Terrestre* for solo piano; *Earth Music,* educational pieces for cello; and *Tribute to Carmanah* for cello and piano. Everyone living on the West Coast recognizes the area's natural heritage. In her last years Coulthard became preoccupied with preserving the environment. Protests against the logging of British Columbia's old-growth forests struck her as proof that young eco-activists recognized the deep value of the unique but fragile West Coast her family had loved so deeply. She felt it appropriate to use the titles of her music to give aid and comfort to the young activists she knew.

Throughout the 1980s and 1990s Coulthard continued to write for her favourite Vancouver ensembles. The results included the cantata based on Earle Birney's *Vancouver Lights* and a *Fanfare Overture.* These were intended to honour her city, but were also gifts to her old musical friends in the Vancouver Bach Choir and its long-time conductor Bruce Pullan. For the Vancouver Academy of Music Orchestra — an ensemble that came close to the conservatory orchestras she had known in eastern Canada and in Europe — she created *Western Shore: Prelude for Strings.*

Finally, there was a late crop of solo works for her own instrument, the piano: her *Second Piano Sonata* (1986), the *Image Astrale*

In her last decade

(1980) and the *Image Terrestre* (1990), and then the last of her baker's dozen of *Preludes* begun almost forty years earlier.

In these works, she paid back her community for long years of support and encouragement, but it was more than that. Coulthard harnessed whatever prestige she had accrued, whatever good feelings might have arisen, to her causes. In her last years she understood the continuity of a long musical life. She kept on lobbying performing ensembles, broadcasters, publishers — the powers-that-be — reminding them of their continuing responsibility to Canadian music and Canadian composers.

Margaret Bruce by L.M.F. Lyttelton

THE MUSIC: *Image Astrale* (1980) & *Image Terrestre* (1990)

The two *Images* date from 1980 and 1990 respectively and were composed for two pianist friends of the composer: *Image Astrale* was written "in honour of Cristine Coyiuto," a young pianist from the Philippines who came to live in Vancouver during the 1970s. *Image Terrestre* was the last in a series of pieces for Margaret Bruce, an old family friend and Vancouver-born pianist who established the "Canadians and Classics" series of concerts in London, England.

The titles link the beginning and the end of the twentieth century. "Image" recalls Debussy's famous set of pieces dating from 1905–1907. But the subtitles *Astrale* "of the stars" and *Terrestre* "of the earth" are late twentieth-century ideas. And despite the ten-year gap in their composition, they are companion pieces exploring a favourite formal idea, the palindrome or arch structure made popular by Bartók.

Image Astrale begins by "floating" harmonies over a pedal chord with evocative space imagery, quasi-aleatory staccato figures derived from a 12-note row, reminiscent of similar patterns in Coulthard's other "space" work, the *Sonata for Two Pianos "Of the Universe."*

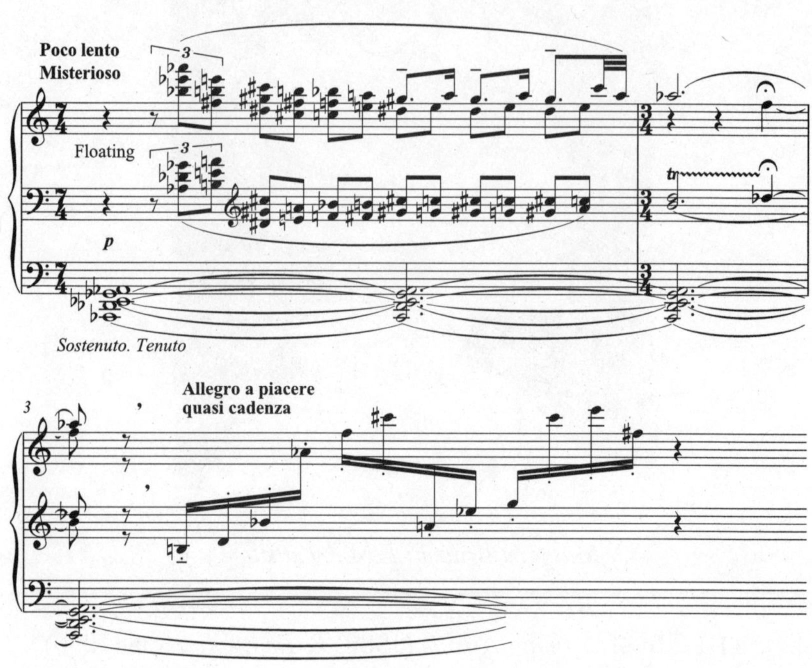

Subsequent sections contrast a "celestial" *tranquillo cantabile* with toccata-like *con brio* passages and *maestoso* chords.

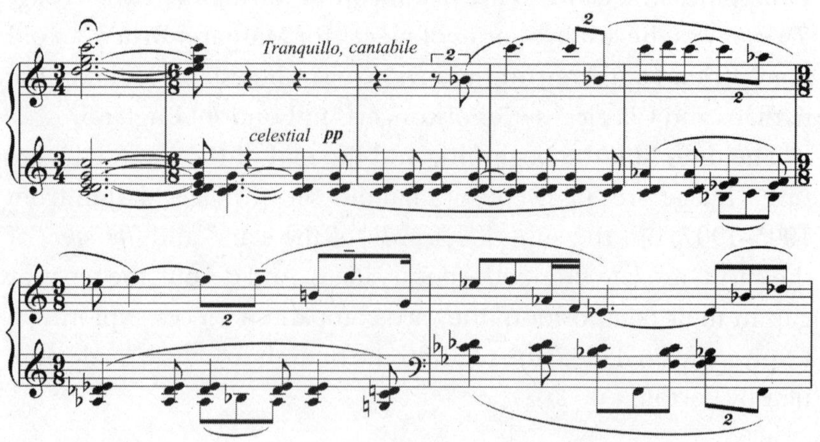

Image Terrestre uses similar materials but is, if anything, a more extroverted and dramatic score. The second *Image* begins *Attacca Allegro drammatico* with a minor/major seventh chord, the same ambiguous sonority that ends the piece.

At the centre of the arch form, *maestoso* chords create a thrilling high-point.

Coulthard's favourite mood and designation is unquestionably lyric, but she was, as always, willing to exploit the technical powers of a well-prepared virtuoso. Like her earlier *Sketches from the Western Woods,* the *Images* are conceived first and foremost as performance pieces: their extroverted style is designed to give the pianist ample opportunity to display a variety of moods and techniques. In *Sketches* her music evokes Emily Carr's eternal western woods: now the environment of *Image Terrestre* is dark and threatened.

Throughout both *Images* Coulthard's emphasis is on the theatrical and the technical, translated into contemporary terms. Coulthard's trick is to make sure that neither piece is all that hard: a well-prepared pianist at an ARCT level can present the works with great effect.

As always Coulthard's piano idiom derives from the great nineteenth- and twentieth-century traditions of keyboard writing. But a few extended techniques display late twentieth-century idioms. A particularly effective moment in *Image Astrale* occurs when Coulthard uses a tone cluster as a dark gong-like sonority underscoring and amplifying *maestoso* chords.

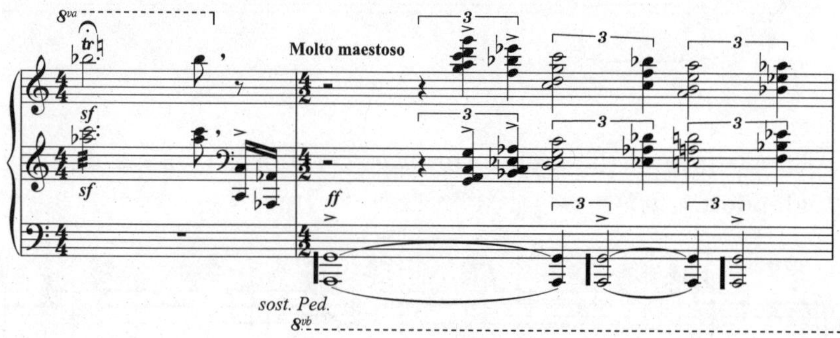

In the final years of her long career Coulthard was secure in her technique and individuality. Her willingness to take risks and to explore new ideas marks the two *Images*. On one level their spirit remains true to Coulthard's "hero gods" at the century's beginning. But her new sounds — from 12-note themes, tone clusters, and modestly minimalist patterns — infuse these two works with a spirit of adventure.

In 1990 Coulthard's daughter Jane, her husband Andreas, and their daughter Alexa relocated from Montreal to West Vancouver and took over the townhouse in Caulfeild Cove. Coulthard downsized one last time to a Bellevue Street apartment in West Vancouver. Where a half-century earlier there had been a handful of summer cottages, now there was a gigantic highrise, known locally as the "Pink Palace." In her new comfortable, airy space, she had room for her mother's grand piano and enjoyed a spectacular view of English Bay. At age eighty-two, she felt blessed to have her family's quiet support and a form of independence.

Younger people who met Coulthard only casually found her gracious and patrician, a holdover, perhaps, from an earlier and gentler era. They did not know the "gracious" persona masked a shy and resilient woman of defined tastes and dry wit.

Since her teenage days, Coulthard had loved clothes. In old age she maintained her standards: fairly severe and tailored in the afternoon, with a touch of a performer's theatricality for evening receptions or concerts.

She walked every day, often accompanied by Lily, her daughter's golden retriever. As she neared her nineties, she accepted that she

Tea time

should stop driving. Her bad eye (a detached retina) and her slightly uncertain balance made it too risky. Perhaps the biggest blow was the loss of her sister in 1997.

> Babs died on a Sunday night. And the most extraordinary thing, on Friday she was here for tea and said to me, "Jeannie, isn't it wonderful that we've got each other. . . ." And it was true, you know. We just saw each other every day. We'd take our lunch out and picnic down by the ocean here. (JC/WB, 10 December 1997)

Babs and Jeannie

Still her musical journey continued. Young professionals discovering Coulthard's earlier works were often surprised by her generosity. Almost always new compositions were written to help a singer, to encourage a favourite harpist or pianist or cellist, or to stimulate performances of Canadian music at home and abroad.

It is too early to tell if the huge volume of her work-in-retirement will become basic repertory in this country or abroad. Still, the insight and the power of the music suggests it has a long life yet to come. With publication, broadcasts, and recording, the Coulthard legacy can only grow. Never one to talk at length about her aesthetics or "philosophy" of composition, Coulthard felt privileged to have had a life as an artist. When pressed, she would claim to agree with Canadian poet A.J.M. Smith, who wrote: "No matter how disillusioned or bitter an artist's philosophical outlook may be, it is always delight and love that are at the heart of his writing." Coulthard added, "And I would say this is definitely so in my experience." (MWL)

The closest she came to expressing a formal artistic credo came in a statement made in the 1970s:

> I have written many kinds of musical composition and in them all my aim is simply to write music that is good. In this great age of scientific development, I feel that human values remain the same and that unless music is able to reach the heart in some way, it loses its compelling power to minister to human welfare. I also think that a composer's musical language should be instinctive, personal, and natural to him, and not to be forced in any way as to the specific style or technique of the moment. For if one becomes over-involved in the mechanics of one's musical thought, inspiration is easily lost. (MWL)

Coulthard believed in inspiration and in individuality but not in academic fads or fashions. She believed tradition mattered and that the creative artist had a responsibility to society.

Age had its advantages. It conferred the power to do good, in artistic and moral terms as she understood them. Few composers outlive their worst critics, and begin to experience their own fame. Not many composers are members of the Order of Canada (1978) and the provincial equivalent (the Order of British Columbia, 1994), as well as Honorary Doctors of their own and other universities (UBC, 1988; Concordia, 1990). Coulthard lived long enough to enjoy these honours, and to make use of them in pressing her causes: Canadian music, the CBC, the Canadian Music Centre, the environment, and Canadian culture generally.

A **Celebration** in **Honour** of

Jean Coulthard:

- Her contributions as one of Canada's finest composers
- Her career as a distinguished faculty member at UBC
- Her generous donation of materials for the study of her music
- Her 90th birthday!

February 10th, 1998
Main Library, The University of British Columbia

(Illustration taken from a painting of Jean Coulthard by her daughter Jane Adams, then age 9, in 1953.)

Ninetieth-birthday Celebration Program, with Janey's first portrait of her mother

For her ninetieth-birthday celebrations, her old University pulled out the stops and gave Coulthard a massive party. The official excuse was the family's decision to donate the entire Coulthard manuscript collection to UBC, complete with rare recordings and the raw materials that had produced all that music across more than eight productive decades. Jean did not exactly see the point of preserving all her rough work and professional papers: "What possible use is all that old stuff?" Historians, archivists, and musicologists disagreed.

University President Martha Piper came to the party, as did Coulthard's old friends from the CBC, the Festival circuit, performers, and students young enough to be her grand- and great-grandchildren. The CBC matched the University's festivities with two large broadcast tributes, and by the end of that ninetieth year, a dozen recitalists had featured her work across the continent.

Coulthard's rule had been to attend performances of her works whenever and wherever possible. By 1999, this applied only to the Vancouver area, and only to selected performances. The Vancouver Symphony Orchestra gave regular performances of Coulthard works under Sergiu Commissiona, and Coulthard was nearly always there. And with the encouragement of Rodney Sharman,

Coulthard's last completed composition

composer-in-residence, and the discreet pressure of musical luminaries outside the Symphony's inner circle, the Orchestra organized the Coulthard Readings, an annual performance of new works by promising young composers.

By the end of the twentieth century, Coulthard's health was such that composition could be only erratic and occasional. The solo cello sonata was finished.[30] She also talked of new songs, and possibly an unaccompanied viola sonata. By early 2000, she felt unable to live alone, even with her network of friends and the consistent support of her daughter and family.

Almost immediately after her ninety-second birthday she suffered a stroke, then quickly deteriorated in hospital. Jean Coulthard died peacefully on March 9, 2000.

That spring, two extraordinary events brought together Coulthard's family and friends in two quite different memorial gatherings. The first was a musical *conversazione* on CBC, held in CBC-Vancouver's Studio One. This studio had been the locus of dozens of broadcasts of Coulthard's music over the years. She had known it well, and so did the performers and friends who came together to celebrate and to mourn. The broadcast was a true "conversation" among friends, musicians, a critic or two, broadcasters, and performers. Coulthard would have loved it.

A few days later, the family and friends gathered on Eagle Island, in West Vancouver, a West Coast place touched by ocean and sky. Coulthard's nephews Tim and John Brock have homes there, and on a fine, warm April day, over two hundred came to talk and to remember Jean Coulthard's long life as a creator, friend, teacher, and beloved family member. Brian Mix performed an excerpt from her last work, the *Sonata* for solo cello.

Both events included Coulthardian touches: music, tea, flowers (always Coulthard looked for flowers — they are everywhere in her music), and, of course, the people she loved.

Jean Coulthard by Andreas Poulsson

8

OVERVIEW

Jean Coulthard composed music regularly for eighty-five of her ninety-two years, completing over 350 distinct works (excluding those withdrawn or radically revised).

It is instructive to put her long creative life in perspective. She was born just over a decade after the deaths of Brahms and Clara Schumann. Mahler's and Debussy's careers ended before she was ten. She was part of a generation of composers born between the turn of the twentieth century and World War I: Francis Poulenc, Benjamin Britten, Dmitry Shostakovich, Aaron Copland, Samuel Barber, and her exact contemporaries Elliott Carter and Olivier Messiaen. She learned and benefited artistically from the music of Debussy and Bartók, Vaughan Williams and Schoenberg, Lutosłavsky and Penderecki. She lived long enough to hear and appreciate the advanced serialism of Pierre Boulez, the African-influenced minimalism of Steve Reich, and the combined eastern *and* western sensibilities in the work of Canadian Alexina Louie.

Over this extended career she attracted her fair share of negative criticism, some deserved. Part of her output was performed and forgotten, some simply neglected and never performed. That having been admitted, Coulthard's catalogue contains undoubted jewels, of which only a fraction are recorded.

In her lifetime, her music was played by such distinguished exponents as the late pianists Marie-Aimée Varro, John Newmark, and John Ogdon; violinist Ruggiero Ricci; cellists Janos Starker and Ernst Friedlander; and singers Maureen Forrester, John Boydon, Phyllis Mailing, Jon Vickers, Pierrette Alarie, and Léopold Simoneau.

Moreover, today's performers find Coulthard's works attractive. CDs of her music are regularly released, and it is impossible to keep up with performances and broadcasts throughout the world.

Despite Coulthard's work as a university theory teacher, she was never especially happy analyzing her own music. She resisted elaborate discussions about her various styles and periods. Scholars found her elusive on these questions. She thought her job was to write the music. It was up to others to offer analysis and evaluation. Her reticence did not prevent a wave of master's and doctoral theses on her works.[31]

In the last decades of her life, Coulthard's reputation was significantly enhanced by growing interest in women who composed. Coulthard always made it clear that her perspective was obviously that of a woman. This shows in many works — the duets *Songs from the Distaff Muse, Music to St. Cecilia,* and *The Christina Songs*. Possibly the use of the term "lyric" in so many compositions could be seen as representative of a female outlook. But as to specific "female" or, for that matter, "male" characteristics of composers, Coulthard demurred.

She acknowledged a fundamental duality in her two streams of music. To this we should add a second duality: her relative isolation in British Columbia and her fondness for the cultural and musical legacy of Europe. She spoke of the joy and affirmation of creation but also the fragility and impermanence of life.

Coulthard especially resisted sharp divisions of her career into early, middle, and late periods. She considered only a handful of compositions from the period before 1939 *(Cradle Song, Threnody, Variations on Good King Wenceslas)* good enough for her official catalogue.

From the late 1930s until the mid-1940s she produced significant works — the orchestral composition *Ballade "A Winter's Tale"*, the ballet *Excursion, Convoy, Music on a Quiet Song* and the piano *Etudes.* These are transitional pieces with style elements derived from English and French early-modern repertoire, marked by occasional forays into more advanced harmony.

With the "sonata year" of 1946–1947 comes a new sense of authority. Coulthard's studies with Bernard Wagenaar encouraged her to combine traditional formal schemes with extended tonal harmonies. Especially important works from this phase of her life include the *Variations on BACH,* the *First Piano Sonata* (Coulthard's first piece performed in Carnegie Hall), the *Duo Sonata* for violin and piano, *Spring Rhapsody,* and the *Violin Concerto.*

After 1960 Coulthard sharpened the distinction between what she called her "two styles." There were genial works designed for the greater musical audience, and those for specific performers and students — *The Bird of Dawning Singeth All Night Long,* the *Piano Concerto, Fantasy* for violin, piano and chamber orchestra, *Two Night Songs,* and *Aegean Sketches.* There were also more personal, abstract works — the *Second* and *Third String Quartets,* and the *Octet: Twelve Essays on a Cantabile Theme*).

Upon her retirement from UBC, Coulthard began a period of increased productivity. The gap between her "two styles" narrowed and she began an exploration of ideas and idioms from post-serial music: quotation, microtonal effects, cluster chords and the like, but always integrated into a recognizable Coulthard idiom. Her final two decades of composition produced such fresh, even experimental works *Image Astrale* and *Image Terrestre,* the *Sonata* for violin and cello, the *Autumn Symphony* for strings, *Shelley Portrait,* and the *Sonata* for solo cello.

Jean Coulthard understood and loved the grand sweep of musical tradition from Palestrina to Penderecki. She sustained her singular voice through nine decades, travelling far in music and in life.

"Whether I am writing a little teaching piece or a long and complicated work, love and delight is for me the heart of it."

Jean Coulthard

JEAN COULTHARD: LIFE AND TIMES

LIFE / COMPOSITIONS		CONTEXT	
1871	September 26: Walter Livingstone Coulthard (1871–1937), b. Gananoque, Ontario, then raised in Picton, Ontario	1872	Ralph Vaughan Williams, b. England
		1875	Arnold Schoenberg, b. Austria
			Maurice Ravel, b. France
1882	August 13: Jean Blake Robinson (1882–1933), b. Moncton, New Brunswick	1882	Béla Bartók, b. Hungary
		1884	Official banning of potlatch in British Columbia; revoked only in 1951
		1885	Last Spike in construction of the Canadian Pacific Railway
		1886	City of Vancouver incorporated
1890	Walter Coulthard matriculates at the University of Toronto in Science, then moves to the Faculty of Medicine	1891	Sir John A. Macdonald, first Prime Minister of Canada, dies

	LIFE / COMPOSITIONS		CONTEXT
		1892	Darius Milhaud, b. France
		1893	Arthur Benjamin, b. Australia
		1894	Debussy, *L'après-midi d'un faune*
1898	Rev. J. Millen Robinson, maternal grandfather of Coulthard, moves with family to Rossland, British Columbia		
1899	Dr. Walter Coulthard moves from Toronto, Ontario to Rossland, British Columbia to practise medicine		
		1900	Aaron Copland, b. USA
1901	Jean Blake Robinson studies music at Boston's New England Conservatory of Music	1901	POPULATION OF VANCOUVER: 27,010
1904	January 12: Marriage of Dr. Walter Coulthard and Jean Blake Robinson, parents of Jean Coulthard		
1905	Dr. and Mrs. Coulthard settle in Vancouver, British Columbia Elizabeth Poston born, England		
1908	January 17: Donald Marvin Adams, future husband of Coulthard, b. Victoria, British Columbia February 10: Jean Coulthard, b. Vancouver, British Columbia	1908	Elgar, *Symphony No. 1* Debussy, *Children's Corner* Ravel, *Gaspard de la nuit* Bartók, *String Quartet No. 1* Vaughan Williams, *Fantasia on a Theme of Thomas Tallis* Debussy, *Preludes, First Set*
1911	Margaret ("Babs") Isobel Coulthard, sister, b. Vancouver	1911	POPULATION OF VANCOUVER: 142,215
		1912	Schoenberg, *Pierrot Lunaire*
1913	Coulthard family moves to 1511 Marpole Street, Shaughnessy Heights, Vancouver Jean Coulthard begins music lessons with mother	1913	Stravinsky, *Rite of Spring* Debussy, *Jeux* Benjamin Britten, b. England
1914	September: Jean Coulthard begins elementary school	1914	Outbreak of World War I Vaughan Williams, *The Lark Ascending*

	LIFE / COMPOSITIONS		CONTEXT
	COMPOSITIONS: 1917–1920 *Early Pieces* *Piping Down the Valleys Wild*	1917	Bartók, *String Quartet No. 2* Ravel, *Le tombeau de Couperin* Debussy, *Violin Sonata*
		1918	World War I ends
			Debussy dies
1919–1920	Mrs. Coulthard, J.C., and Babs to Wellsburg, West Virginia; mother takes voice and piano lessons in New York		Women's suffrage in Canada
			POPULATION OF VANCOUVER: 220,503
1922	J.C. begins occasional piano studies with Jan Cherniavsky and musical theory with Frederick Chubb		
		1924	Holst, *Choral Symphony*
			E.M. Forster, *A Passage to India*
1925	J.C. enrolls at the University of British Columbia in the Faculty of Arts as part-time student; leaves at end of autumn term	1925	Pierre Boulez, b. France
		1926	Bartók, *Piano Concerto No. 1*
		1927	Holst, *Egdon Heath: Homage to Hardy*
1928–1929	J.C. wins Vancouver Women's Musical Club Scholarship	1928	Ravel, *Boléro*
	COMPOSITIONS: 1929 *Cradle Song*		Supreme Court of Canada rules women are not "persons," thus not eligible for public office; Privy Council of Britain in 1929 reverses ruling and women acquire full right to hold public office
	Enrolls in London's Royal College of Music.	1929	October 28: "Black Friday," Stock Market crashes
	Studies with Ralph Vaughan Williams		
	Visits Germany; hears early performance of Hindemith's *Cardillac* (opera); in France July 1929; returns to Vancouver end of summer 1929		
1930–1933	Teaches piano; continues studies in theory with Frederick Chubb; intensifies formal piano study with Jan Cherniavsky	1930	Copland, *Piano Variations*

LIFE / COMPOSITIONS		CONTEXT	
1931	Receives LRSM (Licentiate, Royal Schools of Music) April 21: début recital, Hotel Vancouver	1931	POPULATION OF VANCOUVER: 334,389
1933	July 16: mother dies Receives Associateship of Toronto Conservatory of Music COMPOSITIONS: 1933 *Threnody*, text Robert Herrick: ". . . Now all beauty lies asleep"	1933	Schoenberg leaves Germany Hitler becomes Chancellor of Germany, quickly assumes total power
1934–1936	Teaches piano and theory at St. Anthony's College. Conducts Vancouver Little Theatre Orchestra COMPOSITIONS: 1934 *Variations on Good King Wenceslas*	1934	Bartók, *String Quartet No. 5* Hindemith, *Mathis der Maler* (opera)
1935	December 24: marries Donald Marvin Adams	1935	W.L. Mackenzie King elected Prime Minister of Canada
1936–1937	Teaches piano and theory at the Queen's Hall School for Girls December: J.C. and Don Adams visit Mr. & Mrs. J. Robinson (maternal grandparents) in New York; J.C. studies with Copland	1936	Bartók, *Music for strings, percussion, and celesta* Canadian Broadcasting Corporation (CBC) established Joseph Stalin's regime bans performance of Shostakovich's opera *Lady Macbeth of Mtsensk*
1937	June 6: father dies October: J.C. and Don Adams move to Sperling (now Wiltshire) Street Babs and husband David Brock (1910–1968) travel to Europe	1937	Ravel dies Nazi regime holds exhibition of so-called "degenerate art and music" — including works by Hindemith and Alban Berg, and paintings by Picasso and Kandinsky Guernica, Spanish town, bombed during Spanish Civil War; Picasso makes famous painting of that name
		1938	Vaughan Williams, *Serenade to Music (Shakespeare)*, orchestral-choral version of original choral work

	LIFE / COMPOSITIONS		CONTEXT
1939	Arthur Benjamin settles in Vancouver	1939	World War II begins September Britten comes to Canada, then to the United States; Stravinsky relocates to U.S.
1940	Arthur Benjamin encourages composition of Coulthard works for orchestra COMPOSITIONS: 1940 *Canadian Fantasy* *Excursion*	1940	Milhaud accepts appointment at Mills College, California Bartók and Hindemith emigrate to U.S.
		1941	POPULATION OF VANCOUVER: 388,687 Emily Carr publishes *Klee Wyck* Shostakovich, *Leningrad Symphony*
1942	Coulthard travels to California for criticism lessons with Milhaud and Schoenberg Don Adams enlists in the Royal Canadian Navy COMPOSITIONS: 1942 *Two Songs of the Haida Indians*	1941–1944	The Battle of the North Atlantic
1943	May 24: daughter Jane Adams born		
1944	To New York to stay with grandmother Mrs. Robinson; winter of study with Bernard Wagenaar; studies briefly with Bartók COMPOSITIONS: 1944 *Convoy* *Ballade* "A Winter's Tale"	1944	Bartók, *Concerto for Orchestra*
1945	May: reunited with Don Adams in Saint John, NB. June: family returns to Vancouver COMPOSITIONS: 1945 *Two Sonatinas for Violin and Piano* *Four Etudes*	1945	Bartók dies European theatre of war closes with Allied victory VE Day, May 11 U.S. drops atomic bomb on Hiroshima, Japan
1946	University of British Columbia opens Department of Music, Harry Adaskin named Head and Professor	1946	Winston Churchill denounces Soviet Union and the creation of an "Iron Curtain"

LIFE / COMPOSITIONS		CONTEXT	
1946	CAPAC award to J.C. for *Four Etudes for Piano* COMPOSITIONS: 1946 *Three Songs* (texts by Joyce) *Music on a Quiet Song* *Sonata for Cello and Piano*	1946	International Summer Courses for New Music, Darmstadt established; participants will include Berio, Boulez, Stockhausen, and others
1947	CAPAC award to J.C. for *Sonata for Cello* September 15: appointed Lecturer, Department of Music, University of British Columbia COMPOSITIONS: 1947 *Poem* *Sonata for Piano* *Three Shakespeare Sonnets*	1947	Vaughan Williams, *Symphony No. 6*
1948	Receives Honourable Mention, 14th Olympiad (London), for *Sonata for Oboe and Piano* Meets British composer Elizabeth Poston COMPOSITIONS: 1948 *Sonata for Oboe and Piano* *Quebec May* *Cycle of Three Love Songs*	1948	Introduction by Columbia Records of long-playing 33⅓-RPM recordings, primarily intended for classical music Earle Birney (1904–1995), professor of English at UBC 1948–1965, permits J.C. to set his "Quebec May" for choir and two pianos
1949	July: to UK, visits Elizabeth Poston		
1950	March 12–15: J.C. participates in First Symposium of Canadian Music COMPOSITIONS: 1950 *First Symphony*	1950	Copland, *Twelve Poems of Emily Dickinson* POPULATION OF VANCOUVER: 554,188
1951	Harry Adaskin tries to fire J.C. — her position upheld by UBC administration COMPOSITIONS: 1951 *Variations on BACH* *Night Wind*	1951	Schoenberg dies Canadian League of Composers holds first meeting, Toronto
1952–1956	Don Adams Interiors founded Summer in France		

LIFE / COMPOSITIONS	CONTEXT
1952–1954 J.C. wins Bronze Medal, 15th Olympiad (Helsinki) for *Night Wind*	
COMPOSITIONS: 1952 *First String Quartet* "In the Spring of the Year"	
COMPOSITIONS: 1953 *A Prayer for Elizabeth*	1953 Coronation of Elizabeth II
COMPOSITIONS: 1954 *Three Love Songs*	1954 Lutosławski, *Concerto for Orchestra*
COMPOSITIONS: 1954–1964 *Preludes 1–10*	
1955–1956 Wins fellowship, Royal Society of Canada Year in France Begins opera *The Return of the Native*	
COMPOSITIONS: 1955 *Five Long Songs* (poetry of Emily Dickinson)	
1956 July: family trip to Italy	1956 Hungarian uprising against Soviet occupation, brutally suppressed
COMPOSITIONS: 1956 *Music to Saint Cecilia*	
COMPOSITIONS: 1956–1959 *Concerto for Violin and Orchestra*	
1957 Family moves to 2747 South West Marine Drive, Vancouver. Commissioned by the Vancouver International Festival to write *Spring Rhapsody*	
COMPOSITIONS: 1956–1957 *Piano Quartet* "Sketches from a Medieval Town" *More Lovely Grows the Earth*	
1958 June: to Edinburgh Festival. British premiere of *More Lovely Grows the Earth*	1958 Vaughan Williams dies

LIFE / COMPOSITIONS		CONTEXT	
1958	August: travels to Greece, via Italy COMPOSITIONS: 1958 *The Devil's Fanfare* *Spring Rhapsody*	1958	Centennial of British Columbia mainland's creation as colony; major celebrations, including Vancouver International Festival
	COMPOSITIONS: 1960 *The Bird of Dawning Singeth* *All Night Long* *Two Night Songs*	1960	Arthur Benjamin dies Beginning of Quebec's "Quiet Revolution"
1961	Accompanies daughter Jane to London to begin art school; also represents Canada at Conference of British Women Composers COMPOSITIONS: 1961 *Aegean Sketches* *Fantasy*	1961	January: John F. Kennedy inaugurated President of the United States POPULATION OF VANCOUVER: 796,006
	COMPOSITIONS: 1962 *Sonata Rhapsody for Viola and Piano* *Six Mediaeval Love Songs* *Three Songs*	1962	*Cuban missile crisis* Introduction of cassette tape recording Britten, *War Requiem*
	COMPOSITIONS: 1962–1963 *Concerto for Piano and Orchestra*	1963	John F. Kennedy assassinated
	COMPOSITIONS: 1964–1966 *Second Sonata for Violin and Piano* "A Correspondence" *Music on a Scottish Folk Song* *Six Irish Poems* *Endymion*		
1965–1966	Sabbatical with Gordon Jacob in London, UK. Attends Thurston Dart's lectures on early music at King's College, University of London	1965	Adoption of new Canadian Maple Leaf flag under Prime Minister Lester Pearson
	COMPOSITIONS: 1966 *Ballade of the North*	1966	China's Cultural Revolution, under leadership of Mao Zedong
	COMPOSITIONS: 1966–1968 *Choral Symphony: This Land* (Second Symphony)		Arthur Bliss conducts his *Morning Heroes* with VSO

LIFE / COMPOSITIONS	CONTEXT
	1967 Canadian celebration of Centennial of Confederation
	1968 Worldwide student and labour unrest Martin Luther King assassinated Intensification of Vietnam War Pierre Elliott Trudeau elected Prime Minister of Canada
1969 J.C. in England for the Cheltenham Festival and performance of *Second String Quartet* Summer holiday with family in Spain September 6: Jane Adams marries Andreas Poulsson (b. 1944) COMPOSITIONS: 1969 *Lyric Sonatina for Bassoon and Piano* *The Pines of Emily Carr*	
1970 In England for the Aldeburgh Festival Meets Britten, Mstislav Rostropovich, and Galina Vishnevskaya. Summer in Vienna COMPOSITIONS: 1970 *Sketches from the Western Woods* *Music for Midsummer* *When Music Sounds*	1970 October Crisis in Quebec Crumb, *Ancient Voices of Children*
1971 Summer in England for the Purbeck Festival COMPOSITIONS: 1971 *Lyric Sonatina for Flute and Piano*	1971 POPULATION OF VANCOUVER: 985,689
1972 In England for the Purbeck Festival and the Cheltenham Festival Begins extended Christmas and spring residencies in Honolulu, Hawaii	1972 Lutosławski, *Preludes and Fugue for Thirteen Strings*

LIFE / COMPOSITIONS		CONTEXT	
	COMPOSITIONS: 1972 *Birds of Lansdowne* *Octet: Twelve Essays on a Cantabile Theme* *Songs from the Distaff Muse* (Set I)		
1973	First Okanagan Music Festival for Composers June 30: Retirement University of British Columbia, School of Music COMPOSITIONS: 1973 *Pieces for the Present* *Songs from the Distaff Muse* (Set II)		
1974	Teaches at the Shawnigan Summer School of the Arts September 26: Japanese premiere of *Canada Mosaic* COMPOSITIONS: 1974 *Kalamalka* "Lake of Many Colours" *Canada Mosaic* *Lyric Symphony for Bassoon and Chamber Orchestra* (Third Symphony)	1974	Milhaud dies
1975	In Paris for European premiere of *Sonata Rhapsody for Viola and Piano* April 24: granddaughter Alexa Poulsson born, Montreal COMPOSITIONS: 1975 *Hymn of Creation* *Four Prophetic Songs*	1975	Murder of 2,000,000 civilians in Cambodia under Khmer Rouge regime 1975–1978 Sir Arthur Bliss dies
1976	Returns to the Shawnigan Summer School of the Arts COMPOSITIONS: 1976–1977 *Symphonic Ode for Viola and Orchestra* *Lyric Sonatina for Clarinet and Piano*	1976	Britten dies First Parti Québécois government in Quebec
1977	Gives master classes at the Victoria Conservatory, Victoria, B.C.		

LIFE / COMPOSITIONS

COMPOSITIONS: 1977
Music of Our Time
Three Sonnets of Shakespeare

1978 April: made Freeman of the City of Vancouver

June: Teaches at Banff Centre for the Arts

70th-Birthday Concert featuring Maureen Forrester in Vancouver

Brother-in-law David Brock dies, West Vancouver

COMPOSITIONS: 1978
The Wild Thorn Apple Tree
Fanfare Sonata for Trumpet and Piano
Sonata for Two Pianos "Of the Universe"

1979 Invested as Officer of the Order of Canada

Returns to Banff Centre

COMPOSITIONS: 1979
Three Ballades from the Maritimes
Shizen: Three Nature Sketches from Japan
Sonata for Solo Violin
The Return of the Native
Les chansons du cœur

COMPOSITIONS: 1980
Vancouver Lights: A Soliloquy
Sonatina for flute and bassoon "Pas de deux"
Two Idylls from Greece

COMPOSITIONS: 1981
Third Sonata for Violin and Piano "A la jeunesse"
Image Astrale
A Student's Guide to Musical Form

1982 RCI (Radio Canada International) issues *Anthology* of six long-playing records of J.C. works

CONTEXT

1979 Election of Margaret Thatcher as Prime Minister of the United Kingdom

1981 POPULATION OF VANCOUVER: 1,268,183

Election of Ronald Reagan, President of the United States 1982–1990

IBM launches first personal computer

1982 Compact disks become commercially available

LIFE / COMPOSITIONS		CONTEXT	
1982	Former pupil Chan Ka Nin (b. 1949) appointed to University of Toronto Department of Music COMPOSITIONS: 1982 *Where the Trade Winds Blow* *Songs of a Dreamer*		
1983	J.C. and Don Adams sell property at 2747 South West Marine Drive, Vancouver; move to West Vancouver townhouse Last of regular winter-spring residencies in Honolulu, Hawaii COMPOSITIONS: 1983 *Third String Quartet* *Ballade Of the West* *Dopo Botticelli* *Christina Songs* COMPOSITIONS: 1984 *Lyric Sonatina for Solo Guitar* COMPOSITIONS: 1984–1985 *Autumn Symphony for Strings* (Fourth Symphony) *Cycle of Five Lyrics from the Chinese*	1983	European Union bans import of white seal products after years of protest in Canada and abroad against seal harvest
1985	July 9: Husband Donald Adams dies COMPOSITIONS: 1985 *Frescoes* *Fanfare Overture*		
1986	"Canadians and Classics" series begins, London: *Autumn Symphony*, dir. Peter Gellhorn COMPOSITIONS: 1986 *Second Piano Sonata* *Introduction and Three Folk Songs* *Earth Music* *Preludes 11–13*	1986	Expo 86, World's Fair held in Vancouver, B.C.; Centennial celebration of the City of Vancouver International Whaling Commission bans commercial whale hunt Chernobyl nuclear power plant malfunctions, fallout blankets Europe and the world
1987	Elizabeth Poston dies COMPOSITIONS: 1987 *Shelley Portrait*		

LIFE / COMPOSITIONS		CONTEXT	
1988	June: D. Litt. (hon.), University of British Columbia COMPOSITIONS: 1988 *Serenade* (adapt. of orch. work for viola, strings)		
1989	Last trip to Europe COMPOSITIONS: 1989 *Gardens* *When Tempests Rise* (choral suite; adapt. from opera *The Return of the Native*) *Symphonic Image of the North*	1989	Berlin Wall dismantled Solidarity Movement in Poland rapidly gains ground
1990	Moves to apartment on West Vancouver seaside; daughter and family occupy townhouse COMPOSITIONS: 1990 *Image Terrestre* *Polish Lullaby*	1990	Copland dies, New York Polish government falls
1991	June: LL.D. (hon.), Concordia University, Montreal COMPOSITIONS: 1991 *The Enchanted Island* COMPOSITIONS: 1992 *Three Ancient Memories of Greece* *Voices*	1991	Soviet Union disintegrates POPULATION OF VANCOUVER: 1,602,590
1993	September 23–26: First performance, in concert, of *The Return of the Native,* opera in four acts COMPOSITIONS: 1993 *Three Persian Quatrains* *Of Fields and Forests* *Songs from the Zulu*	1993	First Gulf War
1994	April 28: made member of the Order of British Columbia COMPOSITIONS: 1994 *Celebration Fanfare for Orchestra*	1994	Nelson Mandela, once a political prisoner under Apartheid, elected President of South Africa

	LIFE / COMPOSITIONS		CONTEXT
	COMPOSITIONS: 1995 *Western Shore, Prelude for Strings*	1995	Second Quebec referendum on sovereignty narrowly defeated
	COMPOSITIONS: 1996 *Tribute to Carmanah*	1996	June: Greenpeace protesters blockade a logging operation in Clayoquot Sound, Vancouver Island
1997	September 11: sister Babs Brock dies COMPOSITIONS: 1997 *Legend from the West* *Sonata for Solo Cello*	1997	Hong Kong reverts to Chinese rule Princess Diana of Wales dies in car crash in Paris, France
1998	Vancouver Symphony Orchestra establishes Coulthard Readings for young composers	1998	Initialling of Treaty with Nisga'a First Nation in British Columbia; ratification 2000
1999	Last visit to Hernando Island		
2000	March 9: Jean Coulthard dies in North Vancouver hospital March 10, March 19: CBC commemorative concerts and broadcasts April 16: Family and friends celebrate J.C.'s life on Eagle Island, West Vancouver	2001	POPULATION OF VANCOUVER: 1,986,965

A SELECTION OF JEAN COULTHARD'S MUSIC

A representative sample of Jean Coulthard's music has found its way into print. The list below also includes items available from the Canadian Music Centre (information about the Centre appears after the last item). Our list includes *both* published and unpublished (but readily available) works.

For Keyboard

FOUR ETUDES (1945) Berandol
FIRST PIANO SONATA (1947) Berandol
VARIATIONS ON BACH (1952) Novello
THIRTEEN PRELUDES (1954/86) I-III Berandol; VII Waterloo
AEGEAN SKETCHES (1961) Berandol
SONATA FOR TWO PIANOS "Of the Universe" (1978) CMC
IMAGE ASTRALE (1980) Avondale

SECOND PIANO SONATA (1986) Avondale
IMAGE TERRESTRE (1990) Avondale

For Students

EARLY PIECES for piano (1917–1921) Alberta Keys
PIECES FOR THE PRESENT for piano (1973) Waterloo
MUSIC OF OUR TIME for piano (1977–1980) Waterloo
A STUDENT'S GUIDE TO MUSICAL FORM for piano (1979) Waterloo
A LA JEUNESSE for violin and piano [published title: *Encore Series*] (1980) Frederick Harris
EARTH MUSIC for cello and piano (1986) CMC

For Solo Instrument

SONATA for violin (1979) CMC
LYRIC SONATINA for guitar (1984) CMC
OF FIELDS AND FORESTS for harp (1993) CMC
SONATA for cello (1997) CMC

For Instrumental Duo

SONATA for cello and piano (1946) Novello
SONATA for oboe and piano (1948) Waterloo
DUO SONATA [First Sonata] for violin and piano (1952) Berandol
SONATA RHAPSODY for viola and piano (1962) Waterloo
A CORRESPONDENCE [Second Sonata] for violin and piano (1964)
LYRIC SONATINA for bassoon and piano (1969) Waterloo
LYRIC SONATINA for flute and piano (1971) Waterloo
LYRIC SONATINA for clarinet and piano (1976) CMC
FANFARE SONATA for trumpet and piano (1978) CMC
SHIZEN: THREE NATURE STUDIES FROM JAPAN, for oboe and piano (1979) Novello
A LA JEUNESSE [Third Sonata] for violin and piano (1981) CMC
WHERE THE TRADE WINDS BLOW for flute and piano (1982) CMC
FANTASY SONATA for horn and piano (1983) CMC
GARDENS for clarinet and piano (1989) CMC

For the Stage

EXCURSION [ballet] (1940) CMC
THE DEVIL'S FANFARE [ballet] for 3 dancers, violin and piano (1958) CMC
THE RETURN OF THE NATIVE [opera] (1956–1979) CMC

For Orchestra

CANADIAN FANTASY (1940) Berandol
FIRST SYMPHONY (1950) Berandol
A PRAYER FOR ELIZABETH for string orchestra (1953) Berandol
ENDYMION (1966) Berandol
KALAMALKA (1974) Waterloo
CANADA MOSAIC (1974) Waterloo
AUTUMN SYMPHONY [Fourth Symphony] for string orchestra (1984) CMC

For Soloist and Orchestra

MUSIC ON A QUIET SONG for flute and strings (1946) Waterloo
NIGHT WIND for medium voice and orchestra (1951) CMC
CONCERTO for violin and orchestra (1959) CMC
THE BIRD OF DAWNING SINGETH ALL NIGHT LONG for violin and strings (1960) CMC
FANTASY for violin, piano and chamber orchestra (1961) Berandol
CONCERTO for piano and orchestra (1963) CMC
MUSIC TO SAINT CECILIA for organ and strings (1956–1969) CMC
LYRIC SYMPHONY [Third Symphony] for bassoon and orchestra (1975) CMC
SYMPHONIC ODE for viola and orchestra (1977) CMC

For Choir

THRENODY SATB (1933) Berandol
QUEBEC MAY, for choir and two pianos (1948) Waterloo
MORE LOVELY GROWS THE EARTH SATB (1957) CMC
CHORAL SYMPHONY: *This Land* [Second Symphony] for choir and orchestra (1967) CMC

HYMN OF CREATION for choir and percussion (1975) CMC
VANCOUVER LIGHTS for choir and orchestra (1980) CMC

For Voice and Piano

CYCLE OF THREE LOVE SONGS (1948) CMC
SPRING RHAPSODY (1958) Waterloo
SIX MEDIEVAL LOVE SONGS (1961) CMC
SIX IRISH POEMS (1964) CMC
CHRISTINA SONGS (1983) CMC
THREE PERSIAN QUATRAINS (1993) CMC

For Voice and Instrumental Ensemble

THREE SHAKESPEARE SONGS for soprano and string quartet (1947) CMC
TWO NIGHT SONGS for baritone, string quartet, and piano (1960) CMC
THE PINES OF EMILY CARR for alto, narrator, string quartet, piano, and timpani (1969) CMC
MUSIC FOR MIDSUMMER for soprano, violin, viola, cello, and harp (1970) CMC
FOUR PROPHETIC SONGS for alto, flute, cello, and piano (1975) CMC
SHELLEY PORTRAIT for alto, flute, clarinet, cello, and piano (1987) CMC

For Chamber Ensembles

FIRST STRING QUARTET "In the Spring of the Year" (1952) CMC
PIANO QUARTET "Sketches from a Medieval Town" (1957) CMC
LYRIC TRIO for violin, cello, and piano (1968) CMC
SECOND STRING QUARTET "Threnody" (1970) Berandol
OCTET: TWELVE ESSAYS ON A CANTABILE THEME, for double string quartet (1972) CMC
THE BIRDS OF LANDSDOWNE for violin, cello, tape, and piano (1972) CMC
THIRD STRING QUARTET (1981) CMC

RECORDINGS ON COMPACT DISK

Coulthard recordings are here organized by

A. name of work, with details of performance and with the publication data for the CD or CDs on which it appears, and by

B. title of CD.

A. Coulthard Recordings, by name of work

Alexa's Music Box

CD: *Canadian Compositions for Young Pianists* (Ottawa, Canada: Studea Musica, 2000). Perf. Elaine Keillor.

Alexa's Bell Song

CD: *Canadian Compositions for Young Pianists* (Ottawa, Canada: Studea Musica, 2000). Perf. Elaine Keillor.

Bird of Dawning Singeth All Night Long, The

CD: *Entre Amis* (Toronto: CBC, 1986). Perf. Cameron Trowsdale, violin, and CBC Vancouver Orchestra, cond. Mario Bernardi.

CD: *Canadian and American Music for Chamber Orchestra* (Toronto: CBC, 1997).

CD: *Ovation, vol. I* (Toronto: CBC Records, 2002).

CD: *Best of Christmas at the Cathedral, vol. 2* (Sioux Falls, South Dakota, USA: Catholic Foundation of Eastern South Dakota, 2004).

Burlesca for Piano and String Orchestra

CD: *Divertimenti* (Surrey-on-Thames, UK: Canadians and Classics, 1996). Perf. Margaret Bruce, cond. P. Gellhorn

Concerto for Piano and Orchestra

CD: *Portraits: Canadian Composers* (Toronto: CMC Centrediscs, 2002). Perf. Silverman/CBC Vancouver Orchestra cond. Dwight Bennett).

i. Allegro ma non troppo; ii. Arioso: semplice;
iii. Finale: allegro marcato

CD: *Living Music 2003* (Toronto: CMC 2002).

Contented House, The

CD: *Tableau* (Montreal: CBC Enterprises, 1989). CBC Vancouver Orchestra, cond. Mario Bernardi.

CD: *Introduction to Canadian Music* (London: Naxos, 1996).

Cradle Song

CD: *Love Came Down at Christmas* (Toronto: Independent, 2002). Perf. Stacey Clark.

"Ecstasy," from *Spring Rhapsody*

CD: *Canadian Classical Songs* (Toronto: Gemstone, 1997). Perf. David Mills and Marjorie Mutter.

Excursion Ballet Suite

CD: *Down Under* (Montreal: CBC Enterprises, 1990). Perf. Symphony Nova Scotia, cond. Georg Tintner.

i. The Seagull; ii. Polka; iii. Summer Romance;
iv. Bicycle Parade; v. The Departure.

CD: *Colonial Diversions: Orchestral Miniatures by Grainger, Lilburn, Benjamin and Coulthard* (London: Naxos, 2004). Symphony Nova Scotia, cond. Georg Tintner.

Fanfare Sonata for Trumpet

CD: *The Trumpet Comes of Age* (Camas, Washington: Crystal Records, 1996). Perf. Louis Ranger and Bruce Vogt.

i. Con vivo, allegro ma non troppo ii. Passacaglia

"Far beyond all Dreams," from *Six Mediaeval Love Songs*

CD: *Art Song Heritage of the Americas.* (Broomall, Pennsylvania: CRS, 1996). Perf. Frederick Kennedy and Henri Venanzi.

Far Above the Clouds

CD: *Canadian Compositions for Young Pianists* (Ottawa, Canada: Studea Musica, 2000). Perf. Elaine Keillor.

First Piano Sonata

CD: *Views of the Piano Sonata* (Ottawa: Carleton University, Department of Music, 1998). Perf. Elaine Keillor.

i. Freely and lyrically; ii. Threnody: Slow and pensively; iii. Finale: Resolutely .

CD: *Motions & Emotions* (n.p.: Echiquier Records: 2004). Perf. Mary Kenedi.

Four Irish Songs

CD: *Linda Maguire Sings* (Toronto: CBC, 1995). Perf. Linda Maguire. CBC Vancouver Orchestra, cond. Mario Bernardi.

i. The White Rose; ii. Innocence; iii. Cradle Song; iv. Frolic.

Gardens

CD: *The Concordia Commissions, vol. I: Music, when soft voices die, vibrates in the memory* (Montreal: SNE, 1996 June). Perf. Sherman Friedland and Dale Barlett.

i. The Royal Garden; ii. The Secret Garden; iii. The Wild Garden.

Grandfather Clock

CD: *Canadian Compositions for Young Pianists* (Ottawa, Canada: Studea Musica, 2000). Perf. Elaine Keillor.

Happy Photographer, The

CD: *Canadian Compositions for Young Pianists* (Ottawa, Canada: Studea Musica, 2000). Perf. Elaine Keillor.

Image Astrale

CD: *Ballade* (Toronto: Centrediscs, 1991). Perf. Charles Foreman.

Introduction and Three Folk Songs

CD: *Tableau* (Montreal: CBC Enterprises, 1989). CBC Vancouver Orchestra, cond. Mario Bernardi.

i. Introduction: Lullaby for a Snowy Night;
ii. Mam'zelle Québécoise; iii. The Contented House; and
iv. Blowing Fields of Golden Wheat.

CD: *Ovation, vol. I* (Toronto: CBC Records, 2002).

Jack Hammer, The

CD: *Canadian Compositions for Young Pianists* (Ottawa, Canada: Studea Musica, 2000). Perf. Elaine Keillor.

Little Joke, A

CD: *Canadian Compositions for Young Pianists* (Ottawa, Canada: Studea Musica, 2000). Perf. Elaine Keillor.

Lullaby for Christmas

CD: *Love Came Down at Christmas* (Toronto: Independent, 2002). Perf. Stacey Clark.

Lullaby for a Snowy Night

CD: *Special Edition, vol. II* (Montreal: CBC Enterprises, 1989). Perf. CBC Vancouver Orchestra, cond. Mario Bernardi.

Lyric Sonatina for Flute and Piano

CD: *Fabulous Femmes* (Bâton Rouge, LA: Centaur Records, 2000). Perf. Athena Trio.

i. Moderato; ii. Poco lento;
iii: Allegro ma non troppo (Caprice).

"Mam'zelle Québécoise," from *Introduction and Three Folk Songs*

CD: *The Stereo Morning Collection* (Toronto: CBC, 1996).

Mathematician

CD: *Canadian Compositions for Young Pianists* (Ottawa, Canada: Studea Musica, 2000). Perf. Elaine Keillor.

Music on a Quiet Song

CD: *Concierto Pastoral* (Toronto: Canadian Broadcasting Corporation, 1998). Perf. Timothy Hutchins and CBC Vancouver Orchestra, cond. Mario Bernardi.

CD: *Ovation, vol. I* (Toronto: CBC Records, 2002).

Music to St. Cecilia for Orchestra

CD: *Women Write Music: Orchestral Music by 20th Century Women Composers* (Outremont, Quebec: ATMA Records, 1999). Foundation Philharmonic Orchestra, cond. David Snell.

Music to St. Cecilia for Organ and Strings

CD: *20th Century Organ Concertos* (Toronto: CBC, 1992). Perf. Patrick Wedd and Calgary Philharmonic Orchestra, cond. Mario Bernardi.

"New Love," from *Six Mediaeval Love Songs*

CD: *Art Song Heritage of the Americas* (Broomall, Pennsylvania: CRS, 1996). Perf. Frederick Kennedy and Henri Venanzi.

"O Lovely Venus," from *Six Mediaeval Love Songs*

CD: *Art Song Heritage of the Americas* (Broomall, Pennsylvania: CRS, 1996). Perf. Frederick Kennedy and Henri Venanzi.

Octet: Twelve Essays on a Cantabile Theme

CD: *Portraits: Canadian Composers* (Toronto: CMC Centrediscs, 2002). Perf. University of Alberta String Quartet and Purcell String Quartet.

Of Fields and Forests, a Roundelay for Harp

CD: *Of Fields and Forests* (Toronto: CBC Records, 1998). Perf. Rita Costanzi.

CD: *Ovation, vol. I* (Toronto: CBC Records, 2002).

Prelude No. 4 for Piano

CD: *Canadian Compositions for Young Pianists* (Ottawa, Canada: Studea Musica, 2000). Perf. Elaine Keillor.

Quebec May

CD: *Elmer Iseler Singers* (Toronto: CBC Records, 1992). Perf. Elmer Iseler Singers, CBC Vancouver Orchestra, cond. Elmer Iseler.

CD: *Glick, Holman, Somers and Others* (Toronto: CBC, 1997). Perf. Elmer Iseler Singers, CBC Vancouver Orchestra, cond. Elmer Iseler.
CD: *Ovation, vol. I* (Toronto: CBC Records, 2002).

Rocking Chair, The
CD: *Canadian Compositions for Young Pianists* (Ottawa, Canada: Studea Musica, 2000). Perf. Elaine Keillor.

"Sarabande" from *Sonata for Cello and Piano*
CD: *The New Historical Anthology of Music by Women Composers* (Indiana University Press: 2004), companion compact disc. Perf. William Grubb and Anne Briscoe.

Shelley Portrait
CD: *The Concordia Commissions, vol. I: Music, when soft voices die, Vibrates in the memory* (Montreal: SNE, 1996 June). Perf. Sherman Friedland. Beverley McGuire, Liselyn Adams, Josée Campeau, and Dale Bartlett.
i. Song of Proserpine; ii. The Cloud; iii. To Music; iv. Fragment; v. To a Skylark; vi. Shelley's Skylark.

Six Mediaeval Love Songs
CD: *Vickers: Canadian Art Songs/Chansons canadiennes.* (Toronto: Canadian Music Centre, 1998). Perf. Jon Vickers and R. Woitach.
i. Far Beyond All Dreams; ii. Young and Golden Haired; iii. O Lovely Restless Eyes; iv. New Love; v. Softly the West Wind Blows; vi. O Lovely Venus.

Sketches from the Western Woods
CD: *Jean Coulthard: Portraits: Canadian Composers* (Toronto: CMC Centrediscs, 2002). Perf. John Ogdon.
i. Revelation in the Forest; ii. The Silent Pool; iii. Elements.

Sonata Rhapsody for Viola and Piano
CD: *Sonata Rhapsody for Viola and Piano* (Montreal: SNE, 1988). Perf. Robert Verebes, viola, and Dale Bartlett, piano.
i. Allegro — Attaca dramatico a piacere; ii. Interlude in May — Lento ma non troppo e grazioso; iii. Allegro con brio.

CD: *Sonata Rhapsody for Viola and Piano* (Toronto: CBC, 1994).
Perf. Steven Dann, viola, and Bruce Vogt, piano.

CD: *Portrait of the Viola* (Toronto: Musica Viva: 2001).
Perf. Steven Dann, Bruce Vogt.

Spring Rhapsody

CD: *Ovation, vol. I* (Toronto: CBC Records, 2002).
Perf. Maureen Forrester and John Newmark.
i. Now Great Orion Journeys to the West;
ii. To a May Flower; iii. Admonition for Spring;
iv. Ecstasy.

Star Song, The

CD: *Love Came Down at Christmas* (Toronto: Independent, 2002).
Perf. Stacey Clark

Star Gazing

CD: *Canadian Compositions for Young Pianists* (Ottawa, Canada: Studea Musica, 2000). Perf. Elaine Keillor.

Threnody

CD: *My Soul, There is a Country* (Edmonton: Arktos Recordings, 2002). Perf. University of Alberta Madrigal Singers.

Villanelle (Final movement of *Sonata for Cello and Piano*)

CD: *Salut d'amour* (New York: RCA Victor/BMG, 1990).
Perf. Ofra Harnoy, cello.

B. Coulthard Recordings, by title of CD

Entre Amis (Toronto: CBC, 1986).

Mendelssohn, Martinu, Coulthard (Montreal: SNE, 1988).

Tableau (Montreal: CBC, 1989).

Special Edition, vol. II (Montreal: CBC, 1989).

Down Under: Music from Australia, New Zealand and Canada (Montreal: CBC, 1990).

Salut d'amour (New York: RCA Victor/BMG, 1990).

Ballade (Toronto: Centredisc, 1991).

Patrick Wedd, Organ (Toronto: CBC, 1992).

Elmer Iseler Singers (Toronto: CBC, 1992).

Portrait of the Viola (Toronto: CBC, 1994).

Linda Maguire Sings (Toronto: CBC, 1995).

The Concordia Commissions, vol. I: Music, when soft voices die, vibrates in the memory (Montreal: SNE, 1996 June).

Divertimenti (Surrey-on-Thames, UK: Canadians and Classics, 1996).

The Trumpet Comes of Age (Camas, Washington: Crystal Records, 1996).

Canadian Classical Songs (Toronto: Gemstone, 1997).

Glick, Holman, Somers and Others (Toronto: CBC, 1997).

Vickers: Canadian Art Songs/Chansons canadiennes. (Toronto: CMC, 1998).

Views of the Piano Sonata (Ottawa: Carleton University, Department of Music, 1998).

Of Fields and Forests (Toronto: CBC, 1998).

Concierto Pastoral (Toronto: CBC, 1998).

Women Write Music: Orchestral Music by 20th-Century Women Composers (Outremont, Quebec: ATMA Records, 1999).

Canadian Compositions for Young Pianists (Ottawa, Canada: Studea Musica, 2000).

Fabulous Femmes (Bâton Rouge, LA: Centaur Records, 2000).

Art Song Heritage of the Americas (Broomall, PA.: CRS Master Recordings, 1996).

Jean Coulthard: Portraits: Canadian Composers (Toronto: CMC, 2002).

Ovation, vol. I (Toronto: CBC, 2002).

Love Came Down at Christmas (Toronto: Independent, 2002).

My Soul, There is a Country (Edmonton: Arktos Recordings, 2002)

Best of Christmas at the Cathedral, vol. 2 (Sioux Falls, South Dakota, USA: Catholic Foundation of Eastern South Dakota, 2004).

Motions & Emotions (Toronto: Echiquier Records: 2004).

New Historical Anthology of Music by Women Composers (Indiana University Press: 2004), book with companion compact disc.

PUBLICATIONS AND SOURCES

Two international music encyclopaedias — the *New Grove Dictionary of Music and Musicians* and *Die Musik in Geschichte und Gegenwart* — include substantial entries on the life and work of Jean Coulthard. The *Encyclopaedia of Music in Canada* gives extensive coverage to her.

To help students, researchers, and general readers interested in Coulthard's music and life, and in Canadian music, we offer a list of selected sources and publications.

Our sources include a list of files publicly available in the Archives, Department of Special Collections, Library of the University of British Columbia. Readers looking for primary documents may find helpful our archival summary.

We begin with selected articles and book-chapters, then provide a list of graduate research theses on Coulthard's music, and summarize the rich archives available for Coulthard studies.

Journal articles and chapters in books

Bruneau, William, "With Age the Power To Do Good: Jean Coulthard's Latest Decades," *Classical Music*, vol. 19, no. 2 (June 1996): 14–19.

Bruneau, William. "Music and Marginality: Jean Coulthard and the University of British Columbia, 1947–1973," in E. Smyth, *et al.*, eds., *Challenging Professions: Historical and Contemporary Perspectives on Women's Professional Work* (Toronto: University of Toronto Press, 1999), 96–116.

Bruneau, William. "Jean Coulthard: An Artist's Voyages," *IAWM Journal*, vol. 6, no. 3 (Autumn 2000): 23–28.

Colton, Glenn. "Jean Coulthard and Artist Emily Carr: Spiritual Encounters With Nature," *IAWM Journal*, vol. 4, no. 2 (Winter 1998): 4–9.

Kydd, Roseanne. "Jean Coulthard: A Revised View," in *Sound Notes*, no. 2 (spring/summer 1992): 14–24.

Of related interest:

Duke, David. "Notes towards a portrait of Barbara Pentland," *Music Works*, no. 70 (Spring 1998): 16–20.

Theses for doctoral degrees on Jean Coulthard's music

(In chronological order of completion and defence)

Rowley, Vivienne W. "The Solo Piano Music of Canadian Composer Jean Coulthard," DMA thesis, Boston University, 1973.

Lee, Barbara. "The Solo Piano Works of Jean Coulthard," DMA thesis, Catholic University of America, 1986.

Duke, David Gordon. "The Orchestral Music of Jean Coulthard: A Critical Assessment," PhD thesis, University of Victoria, Victoria, Canada, 1993.

Colton, Glenn D. "The Piano Music of Jean Coulthard," PhD thesis, University of Victoria, Victoria, Canada, 1996.

Maves, Dale P. "The Art Songs for Voice and Piano by Jean Coulthard: An Eclectic Analysis of Selected Songs," PhD thesis, New York University, 1996.

Black, Linda M. "Jean Coulthard and Her Choral Music," PhD thesis, University of Florida, 1997.

Crookall, Christine. "Jean Coulthard's *Sonata for Cello and Piano*: A Confluence of Stylistic Tendencies," DMA thesis, University of Texas at Austin, Austin, Texas, 2001. (Mainly on the *Sonata for Cello and Piano* of 1946.)

Graduate theses partly concerned with Coulthard's music and circumstances

Tong, Daniel. "An Analytical Annotation of Selected Unpublished Canadian Choral Compositions Suitable for Senior High School Choirs: 1987–1990," MMus thesis, Brandon University, Brandon, Manitoba, 1992. (Pages 60–68, Part II, sec. 2, 'Analysis of DIFFICULT [*sic*] Compositions,' on Coulthard's *Polish Lullaby* for chamber choir.)

Cheney, Elliott Ward. "A Survey of Contemporary Canadian Music for Violoncello and Piano," DMA thesis, University of Texas at Austin, Austin, Texas, 1994. (Chapter 4, sec. 10, "Jean Coulthard," 70–76, piece entitled *Dopo Botticelli.*)

Scott, Marilyn Elizabeth. "Too Good to Ignore: The Work of Canadian Women Composers," MA thesis in Education, University of Toronto, 1995. (Extensive discussion of "ghettoization" of women's music in Canada and the United States. No direct discussion of Jean Coulthard's music.)

Archival Resources

The Archives, Department of Special Collections, Library of the University of British Columbia, holds the Coulthard Papers. Detailed inventories for the Coulthard papers appear on the UBC Archives website.

The papers fall into two broad categories.

First, there are twenty-seven cartons of private and family records, including photographic and non-print records, along with sub-series for Coulthard's financial dealings, and sequences of files concerned with concert and recital programs. Papers in the first category occupy Boxes 1–27 and 32–35.

Second, the Coulthard papers provide a complete manuscript and print record of her musical compositions. In more than 80 percent of cases, these files (at Boxes 28–31) include a record of composition from the stage of rough pencilled sketch, to black-line score, to published final music — often with Coulthard's notations and remarks in handwritten marginalia.

A further sub-series includes sound recordings, with a significant number of 78-RPM CBC air-checks, and several dozen 33⅓-RPM long-play recordings.

In 2005, a third major accession of Coulthard papers will extend the first sequence from Box 36 upward. This accession is largely concerned with family records and history, legal matters, and business relations with performers.

COMPLETE CITATIONS FOR ABBREVIATIONS

At page xv, there is a list of *Abbreviations* and brief textual sources for them. Here is a bibliographically complete list:

AYIF "A Year in France"
[Title supplied: "A Year in France."] Talk given to the Vancouver Women's Musical Club, *ca.* 1956. Coulthard Papers, Archives, Department of Special Collections, Library of the University of British Columbia: Box 4, file 26. Seven pages manuscript in Jean Coulthard's hand. Ink, with pencilled revisions

CWS "The Cottage on Wiltshire Street"
From *Six Autobiographical Essays*, manuscript, probably written 1970–1971. Coulthard Papers, Archives, Department of Special Collections, Library of the University of British Columbia.

DYC "Diary of a Young Composer"
Jean Coulthard. MS journal, 30.11.1930 to 26.07.1934.
On lined blanks, 80 leaves, 160 pages. Hardbound in grey card. Cover stamped, "THE HERALDIC SERIES | *Domine dirige nos*" Pages 1–14: notes on orchestration; pages 15–130, "A Private Diary." Coulthard Papers, Archives, Department of Special Collections, Library of the University of British Columbia.

EC "The Eclectic Composer of Today"
Music Magazine, vol. 2, no. 6 (December 1979): 29.

JC/WB Interviews, Jean Coulthard with William Bruneau, 1994–2000. Transcriptions held in Coulthard Papers, Archives, Department of Special Collections, Library of the University of British Columbia.

JMMC Jean Coulthard, "Jean Coulthard and Canadian Music in the 1930s and 1940s," in Beverley Cavanagh, ed. *Canadian Music in the 1930s and 1940s* (Kingston, Ontario: Queen's University, 1986. Proceedings of a Conference held at Queen's University), pp. 26–38.

MWH "Music is My Whole Life"
Transcription of a scripted talk for Radio Canada International on May 20, 1979. No published English text. Oral version recorded in *Anthology of Canadian Music: Jean Coulthard* (Toronto/ Montreal: CBC, 1982), side 1, record 1 (of six long-playing, 33⅓-RPM recordings). French translation in notes, pp. 19–21.

PEC "The Pines of Emily Carr"
Sketch IV from Six Autobiographical Sketches (see above, "CWS")

THYC "Take Heart, Young Composer!"
Scripted radio talk for "This Week," CBC Vancouver, May 29, 1954, 16h04. Original manuscript in Coulthard Papers, Archives, Department of Special Collections, Library of the University of British Columbia: Box 4, file 26.

NOTES

1 [Harry Charlesworth], "The Meaning of Rhythm: Little Jean Coulthard Composes Charming Melody," *The Educator of Canada,* no. 1 (December 1917): 1.

2 [Advertisement], "Mrs. W.L. Coulthard, instructor in latest voice production technique," *Vancouver Daily Province,* September 20, 1920, 8.

3 D. Barry Waterlow, "Frederick Chubb," H. Kallman, *et al.*, eds., *Encyclopaedia of Music in Canada* (Toronto: University of Toronto Press, 1992, 2nd edition), 270. The first movement of Chubb's organ sonata (1939) has been published in the Canadian Musical Heritage series (vol. 19), and recently recorded by Deirdre Piper in Canadian Sounds (Ottawa: Carleton Sounds, 2001), CSCD-1007.

4 Gilles Potvin, "Maurice Ravel au Canada," in J. Beckwith and F.A. Hall, eds., *Musical Canada: Words and Music Honouring Helmut Kallman* (Toronto: University of Toronto Press, 1988), 154.

5 J.B. Gordon, "Impressions of Opera in Germany," *RCM Magazine,* 24, 2 (1928): 42–46; also R.G. Carritt, "More Impressions of Cologne," *RCM Magazine,* vol. 25, no. 2 (1929): 52–54.

6 Jean Coulthard, "A Hidden Diary," in the Coulthard Papers, UBC Archives, Special Collections, Vancouver, Canada, rec. acq., as follows:
I. Jean Coulthard, "A Private Diary," pages 15–130 in MS journal;
II. Jean Coulthard, "Notes on Orchestration," pp. 1–14 in MS journal.

7 At their peak, the list included the Strand, the Capitol, the Paradise, the Lyric, the Plaza, the Dominion, and the Vogue — almost all on Granville's "theatre row." By the twenty-first century, only the Orpheum and the Vogue survived as theatres.

8 Coulthard disowned dozens of these early compositions in later life, but kept the manuscript books. These are now in the Archives, Department of Special Collections, Archives, University of British Columbia.

9 Donald M. Adams, "A Place to Hang My Hat," ms. memoir, copy in Archives, Department of Special Collections, University of British Columbia, pp. 1–2.

10 Harry Adaskin's two-volume autobiography is the standard source on these developments. See Harry Adaskin, *A Fiddler's World: Memoirs to 1938* (Vancouver: November House, 1977), and *A Fiddler's Choice: Memoirs 1938 to 1980* (Vancouver: November House, 1982). On the creation of the Department of Music, see "Music Lecturer Silent on Swing," *Vancouver Sun,* September 24, 1946, 2; "Conservatory of Music Adaskin's Dream for UBC," *Vancouver Daily Province,* September 25, 1946, 7; "Violinist to Give 'Painless' Music Course at University," *Vancouver Daily Province,* October 10, 1946, 25. See also Harry Adaskin, "Finding New Worlds in Music," *Vancouver Sun* Magazine Supplement, October 2, 1948, 3.

11 Bruneau, William. "Music and Marginality: Jean Coulthard and the University of British Columbia, 1947–1973," in E. Smyth, *et al.,* eds., *Challenging Professions: Historical and Contemporary Perspectives on Women's Professional Work* (Toronto: University of Toronto Press, 1999), 96–116.

12 On women's participation in the teaching of music in universities, colleges, conservatories, and normal schools from 1850 on, see William Bruneau, "Music Education," in Linda Eisenmann, ed., *Historical Dictionary of Women's Education in the United States* (Westport, Connecticut: Greenwood, 1998), 283–6. As for teaching and publication on musical analysis in recent times, and the near absence of women from publications in that field, see Janet Danielson, "Five-Sixths of Women Will Stop in the Doll Stage," *Musicworks: Exploration in Sound* no. 81 (Fall 2001): 5–7.

13 See the analysis of the second movement of the *Sonata for Cello and Piano* in James Briscoe, ed., *Anthology of Music by Women Composers* (Bloomington, Ind.: Indiana University Press, 2004).

14 Jamie Bartlett, "Beyond the Apple Tree: The Choral Music of Elizabeth Poston," unpublished DMA thesis, University of Wisconsin, Madison, 1996.

15 Margaret Ashby, *Forster Country* (Stevenage, UK: Flaunden Press, 1991), 131.

16 The British Women Composers Society from 1949 held annual recital series, published occasional newsletters, and in the late 1950s acquired Royal favour. By the turn of the twenty-first century, the Society had given way to several national and regional organizations. The best-known is Women in Music (website: www.womeninmusic.org.uk).

17 Maureen Forrester's own discussion of her career may be found in *Out of Character: A Memoir* (Toronto: McClelland and Stewart, 1986); see also the bibliographical notes in *Encyclopaedia of Music in Canada,* 2nd ed.

18 See Eitan Cornfield, producer, *Portrait: Jean Coulthard* (Toronto: Centrediscs, 2002) for examples.

19 The sketchbooks are now in the Coulthard Papers, Special Collections, University of British Columbia Archives.

20 Personal interview, Jane Adams/William Bruneau, 12 May 1996, West Vancouver, B.C.

21 Coulthard's autobiographical sketch, "The Pines of Emily Carr," provides an extended account. See also Glenn Colton's discussion of Coulthard's response to British Columbian spaces: Glenn Colton, "The Piano Music of Jean Coulthard," PhD thesis, University of Victoria, Victoria, Canada, 1996.

22 The CBC television program *Opening Night* broadcast February 3, 2005 — days before what would have been Coulthard's ninety-seventh birthday — featured performance of *The Pines of Emily Carr.* The broadcast featured the Molinari String Quartet, with solo voice, piano, timpani, and narrator.

23 *Cf.* W. Bruneau, "Music and Marginality."

24 Jean Coulthard, "Canadian Music in the 1930s and 1940s," in Beverley Cavanagh, ed. *Canadian Music in the 1930s and 1940s* (Kingston, Ontario: Queen's University, 1986), 26–38. Proceedings of a Conference held at Queen's University.

25 Jean Coulthard, "The Eclectic Composer of Today," *Music Magazine,* vol. 2, no. 6 (December 1979): 29.

26 Donald M. Adams, "A Place to Hang My Hat," in Coulthard Papers, Archives, University of British Columbia, Rec. Acq. Special Collections, UBC Library.

27 Apart from the UBC website for Coulthard's LLD at that University, see

for Concordia: www.graduatestudies.concordia.ca.

28 Deaville, C. Kenneson, W. Bruneau, *et al.*, "Violet Archer, Jean Coulthard, and Barbara Pentland Remembered," *Canadian Music Review/ Revue de musique des universités canadiennes,* vol. 20, no. 2 (2000): 1–15.

29 For details, see: Kwantlen College website: www.kwantlen.ca.

30 W. Bruneau, "With Age the Power To Do Good: Jean Coulthard's Latest Decades," *Classical Music,* vol. 19, no. 2 (June 1996): 14–19.

31 See "Publications and Sources on the Life of Jean Coulthard," pp. 193–6 of this book.

INDEX

Bold page numbers indicate photograph, illustration, or excerpt from score